MURDER AT THE INN

A BETH SANDERS COZY MYSTERY

A WINDY HOLLOW MYSTERY

IRIS KINGSLEY

"Are you sure about the angle on these, Beth?" Sophie
ed, tilting her head. "Maybe slightly more toward the
ter?"

Before Beth could answer, a furry brown-and-white
sile shot between her legs, nearly sending a tray of
on bars flying. "Snickers!" Beth yelped, grabbing the
e of the table. Her corgi, resplendent in a bright red
dana embroidered with the words "Chief Nibbler"
ded to a halt near a discarded fork, sniffing it with
nse suspicion before letting out a hopeful bark in the
ction of the tarts.

'He's supposed to be moral support, not a trip hazard,"
sighed, bending down to scoop him up. He felt solid
warm against her apron. "And definitely not quality
rol." Snickers wriggled, his oversized ears flopping,
ly disagreeing with her assessment of his duties. The
hadn't even officially opened and already it felt like
ing a tightrope over a pit of falling cutlery and corgi-
ced chaos.

Speaking of quality control, has anyone checked the
tural integrity of Chef Dubois's ego lately?" A whirl-
of auburn curls and brightly patterned scarf
nded upon their booth. Penelope Whittaker – Penny
ner of Pages & Stories bookstore and Beth's closest
l – deposited a steaming travel mug onto a precarious
r of the prep table, narrowly avoiding a bowl of apricot

Because I just overheard him threatening to flambé
Bellwether's prize-winning choux buns if Bellwether's
y encroached one more inch onto his designated terri-
Apparently, booth placement is the new culinary
field." Penny rolled her eyes dramatically, her gaze
ing the bustling room. "Honestly, Beth, the tension

INTRODUCTION

A Critic's Just Desserts… Are Deadly.

Baker Beth Sanders is whisking up delights for Windy
Hollow's prestigious Culinary Expo when infamous critic
Nigel Verner's acid tongue is permanently silenced – found
dead by the dock.

With her own public clash with Verner putting her on the
overbearing police chief's half-baked suspect list, Beth, her
sharp-witted best friend Penny, and ever-loyal corgi
Snickers must sift through a mess of suspects.

Could it be the fiery Chef Dubois, whose temper and
online poison searches are as hot as his flambé? Or elegant
Chef Bellwether, whose past botanical dealings and unique
plant fibers raise more than just eyebrows? Even smooth
investor Julian Croft, whose initialed pen at the scene and a
devastating secret Verner held over him, looks like a recipe
for disaster.

And when Croft's slick PI, Rick Doyle, starts stirring the pot, the recipe for disaster is complete.

Can she piece together the truth before a killer with a taste for vengeance serves her the final course?

ONE

CRASH!!

The jarring clatter of metal on the floor echoed momentarily above the g by a collective intake of breath and a ne

Somewhere near the main entrance looking waiters scrambled to retrieve silverware, their faces flushed. The f Cedar Shore Inn's first Culinary Expo a trapped bee against Beth Sanders's t another notch.

Beth adjusted a stray strand of escaped her ponytail, her fingers smu despite her best efforts. Beside he apprentice, moved with a calm efficie meticulously arranging miniature la silver stand. Each tart, a complex lay crème pâtissière, and delicate, hand sented hours of painstaking work – I small-town baking didn't mean sn chaotic, high-stakes environment.

ask
cer

mis
lem
edg
ban
skid
inte
dire

Beth
and
cont
clea
expo
walk
indu

struc
wind
desc
– ow
frien
corne
glaze

Chef
displa
tory.
battle
sweep

INTRODUCTION

A Critic's Just Desserts... Are Deadly.

Baker Beth Sanders is whisking up delights for Windy Hollow's prestigious Culinary Expo when infamous critic Nigel Verner's acid tongue is permanently silenced – found dead by the dock.

With her own public clash with Verner putting her on the overbearing police chief's half-baked suspect list, Beth, her sharp-witted best friend Penny, and ever-loyal corgi Snickers must sift through a mess of suspects.

Could it be the fiery Chef Dubois, whose temper and online poison searches are as hot as his flambé? Or elegant Chef Bellwether, whose past botanical dealings and unique plant fibers raise more than just eyebrows? Even smooth investor Julian Croft, whose initialed pen at the scene and a devastating secret Verner held over him, looks like a recipe for disaster.

And when Croft's slick PI, Rick Doyle, starts stirring the pot, the recipe for disaster is complete.

Can she piece together the truth before a killer with a taste for vengeance serves her the final course?

ONE

CRASH!!

The jarring clatter of metal on the polished ballroom floor echoed momentarily above the general din, followed by a collective intake of breath and a nervous titter.

Somewhere near the main entrance, a pair of flustered-looking waiters scrambled to retrieve a dropped tray of silverware, their faces flushed. The frantic energy of the Cedar Shore Inn's first Culinary Expo, already buzzing like a trapped bee against Beth Sanders's temples, ratcheted up another notch.

Beth adjusted a stray strand of brown hair that had escaped her ponytail, her fingers smudged with pastry flour despite her best efforts. Beside her, Sophie Tran, her apprentice, moved with a calm efficiency that Beth envied, meticulously arranging miniature lattice tarts on a tiered silver stand. Each tart, a complex layering of spiced apple, crème pâtissière, and delicate, hand-woven pastry, represented hours of painstaking work – Beth's bid to prove that small-town baking didn't mean small-time skills in this chaotic, high-stakes environment.

"Are you sure about the angle on these, Beth?" Sophie asked, tilting her head. "Maybe slightly more toward the center?"

Before Beth could answer, a furry brown-and-white missile shot between her legs, nearly sending a tray of lemon bars flying. "Snickers!" Beth yelped, grabbing the edge of the table. Her corgi, resplendent in a bright red bandana embroidered with the words "Chief Nibbler" skidded to a halt near a discarded fork, sniffing it with intense suspicion before letting out a hopeful bark in the direction of the tarts.

"He's supposed to be moral support, not a trip hazard," Beth sighed, bending down to scoop him up. He felt solid and warm against her apron. "And definitely not quality control." Snickers wriggled, his oversized ears flopping, clearly disagreeing with her assessment of his duties. The expo hadn't even officially opened and already it felt like walking a tightrope over a pit of falling cutlery and corgi-induced chaos.

"Speaking of quality control, has anyone checked the structural integrity of Chef Dubois's ego lately?" A whirlwind of auburn curls and brightly patterned scarf descended upon their booth. Penelope Whittaker – Penny – owner of Pages & Stories bookstore and Beth's closest friend – deposited a steaming travel mug onto a precarious corner of the prep table, narrowly avoiding a bowl of apricot glaze.

"Because I just overheard him threatening to flambé Chef Bellwether's prize-winning choux buns if Bellwether's display encroached one more inch onto his designated territory. Apparently, booth placement is the new culinary battlefield." Penny rolled her eyes dramatically, her gaze sweeping the bustling room. "Honestly, Beth, the tension back there is thicker than Sophie's ganache. You could cut it with a bread knife."

Snickers barked sharply from Beth's arms, as if adding his own commentary on the chef rivalry. Penny reached out to scratch his head. "See? Even the Chief Nibbler agrees. It's practically *War and Peace* back there, but with more butter."

Just as Beth managed a weak smile, a hush fell over their section of the ballroom, a wave of sudden quiet that contrasted sharply with the surrounding clatter. A portly man in an impeccably tailored, dove-grey suit and a rich maple fedora, his face set in lines of perpetual disdain, was bearing down on their station. Nigel Verner. *The* Nigel Verner. His reputation as a culinary critic was legendary, matched only by the trail of ruined restaurants and shattered careers left in his wake.

He stopped directly in front of Beth's display, his eyes – small and sharp behind expensive spectacles – dismissing the careful arrangement with a barely perceptible sniff. He ignored Beth, Penny, and Sophie entirely, his attention fixed on the signature lattice tart. Without a word, he picked one up, examined its intricate weaving with a critical frown, and took a precise, deliberate bite.

The silence stretched. Beth held her breath, Snickers suddenly still in her arms. People in the immediate vicinity were watching with anxiety. Beth saw with rising anxiety the expo photographer capturing the moment.

I hope this doesn't get to TikTok, she thought.

Verner chewed slowly, his expression unreadable. Then, he delicately placed the half- eaten tart back on the silver tray, as if discarding something unpleasant. "My dear," he began, his voice carrying easily in the sudden lull, finally addressing Beth, "this ... confection." He gestured vaguely at the tart. "This kind of faux-nostalgic, homespun nonsense passed off as 'craft baking' should have stayed in your grandmother's flour tin. It's cloying, technically clumsy, and, frankly, demonstrates a profound lack of imagination. It reminds me, rather depressingly, of a similar failure I encountered years ago. Some things are best left in the past."

He gave a final, dismissive flick of his wrist toward her display and turned on his heel, stalking away toward the main stage area, leaving a wake of stunned silence and Beth's cheeks burning. Penny looked ready to explode. Sophie just stared, aghast.

TWO

By mid-afternoon, the Lakeside Ballroom at Cedar Shore Inn had transformed from a scene of setup chaos into the full-throated hum of the Culinary Expo. The air, thick with a complex medley of competing aromas – sizzling garlic and rosemary from one booth, sweet, buttery caramel bubbling in a copper pot at another, the sharp tang of exotic spices drifting from Chef Dubois's flamboyantly presented station – buzzed with excited conversation, the rhythmic chop-chop-chop from demonstration stages, and the cheerful clinking of wine glasses at tasting tables. Bright spotlights illuminated elaborate food displays, turning glistening sauces, intricate vegetable carvings, and perfectly piped creams into edible jewels, almost too perfect to eat.

Beth stood behind her modest Sweets and Treats display table, feeling slightly overwhelmed but determinedly professional. Her honey-fig cake, despite Nigel Verner's earlier scathing dismissal, sat proudly on its stand, flanked by neatly arranged samples of her lavender short-bread and lemon tarts – the catering items she'd managed to salvage and replenish after the morning's disastrous encounter.

She forced a polite smile for passersby, offering tastes and answering questions about her bakery, trying to ignore the lingering sting of Verner's words and the humiliation of the spilled pastry incident. She saw Greta Moffat nearby, adjusting an already perfect floral centerpiece with intense concentration, fretting needlessly about wilting hydrangeas.

NIGEL VERNER himself was making his presence known, sweeping through the aisles like culinary royalty, his sharp fedora a beacon amidst the crowd. He paused dramatically at Chef Rossi's display of traditional Italian pastries, peered down his nose at a cannoli through gold-rimmed spectacles, declared it "tragically limp and, frankly, rather sad," and moved on without tasting, leaving the quiet chef pale and tight-lipped.

He moved on to Chef Dubois's station. His flambé looked exquisite, but Nigel Verner looked on unimpressed. He plucked his tasting fork from his pouch and took a small bite. He chewed it thoughtfully, staring at the ceiling and taking his time, with Dubois's face getting redder and redder. Finally, Nigel swallowed, looked at Chef Dubois and offered blandly: "Undercooked, unsurprisingly from a has-been self- professed culinary star." He dabbed his lips daintily and moved on.

If a man could erupt like Mount Vesuvius, Chef Dubois looked on the verge of spewing molten fury across his meticulously arranged station.

Later, Beth saw him holding court near the wine tasting station, loudly pontificating on the "utter inadequacy" of Californian chardonnays ("Liquid mediocrity!") to a circle of uncomfortable-looking sommeliers. He seemed to thrive on the tension he created, wielding his influence like a weapon, leaving ruffled feathers and bruised egos in his wake.

Amidst the culinary stars and their entourages, the event photographer moved almost invisibly. Beth spotted him occasionally – a glimpse of his camera lens reflecting the light as he captured a chef's intense concentration during a demo, or a quiet shot of guests sampling appetizers. He even stopped by Beth's table briefly, offering a quiet word of encouragement. "Your cake looks beautiful, Ms. Sanders," he murmured, his sympathetic gaze recalling the morning's incident. "The rosettes on the edges ... Did you use a Wilton 2D or Ateco piping tip for those?"

Beth was slightly startled; she might have expected that question from Nigel, but not from a photographer. She looked at his lanyard: *N. Stern.*

"That's an Ateco 846 tip." Beth met his gaze. "You have a good eye, Mr. Stern. Do you bake?"

"Ned, please. No, but I spend more time than is probably healthy at these expos, following chefs and posting their accomplishments. You pick up a thing or two. Your exhibits look fantastic. Don't let Verner get to you. Everyone knows he's mostly hot air and bluster."

He purchased a small box of macarons, paid quickly with precise movements, and melted back into the crowd before Beth could offer more than a grateful, flustered thank you. His quiet kindness felt genuine, a small balm after Verner's public cruelty.

Sophie, having finished replenishing the sample plates at Beth's table, watched the bustling expo scene for a moment, her expression thoughtful.

This glittering world of competitive chefs and sharp-tongued critics was exactly what she had fled.

She remembered the relentless pressure cooker of her Raleigh culinary program – the instructors who valued intricate plating and Instagrammable 'concepts' over fundamental technique, the classmates who seemed more interested in becoming celebrity personalities than skilled artisans. It had felt hollow, a frantic race for "likes" and fleeting trends, leaving her feeling burnt out before her career had even truly begun.

She'd stumbled upon an article online about Sweets and Treats, about Beth Sanders rebuilding her life through her mother's recipes in a small lakeside town, focusing on quality ingredients and time-honored methods. It sounded like an antidote, a return to something real, something nourishing for the soul, not just the feed. Coming to Windy Hollow, working alongside Beth, learning the patient art of perfect puff pastry or the subtle balance of a fruit tart – it felt like finding her way back to why she'd wanted to bake in the first place.

Watching Nigel Verner strut through the ballroom, sowing chaos and hard feelings, only solidified her conviction. She had made the right choice. This quiet corner, this focus on craft and community, was where she belonged, even if it meant facing the occasional collapsed madeleine.

THE FOLLOWING morning broke clear and cool, the chaos of the expo momentarily paused before the second day's events began. Beth, needing to clear her head after the previous day's unpleasantness with Nigel Verner, decided an early walk with Snickers was in order before delivering the morning pastries to the inn. The air by the lake was crisp, smelling sharply of pine needles and damp earth, a welcome contrast to the rich, competing aromas that had saturated the ballroom. Mist still clung to the surface of the water in hazy, ethereal patches, lending the usually cheerful Cedar Shore grounds an air of quiet mystery. The only sounds were the distant cry of a loon and the gentle lapping of water against the shore.

She let Snickers off his leash near the less-frequented path leading toward the old boathouse, trusting him to stay close in the quiet dawn. He immediately put his nose to the ground, tail wagging furiously, investigating the intriguing tapestry of scents left by nocturnal creatures – raccoon, maybe deer, definitely chipmunk.

Beth breathed deeply, enjoying the relative peace, trying to push aside her lingering anxiety about the expo judging later that day. Verner's critique still stung like lemon juice on a paper cut, but she wouldn't let it undermine her confidence in her work.

Her cake was good. Honest. Made with care. That had to count for something, didn't it?

Suddenly, Snickers darted away from the path, ears pricked, letting out a sharp, insistent bark. He ran toward the water's edge near the main dock, stopping abruptly near the pilings, his barking escalating – not his usual playful yaps at squirrels or passing boats, but a series of urgent, almost frantic sounds directed at something near the water. His whole body vibrated with agitation.

"Snickers, come!" Beth called, slightly annoyed, scanning the water for the usual culprits. "Leave it! Those ducks aren't dangerous."

But Snickers ignored her, planting his front paws firmly, barking continuously at something obscured from Beth's view by the angle of the dock and a moored paddleboat. His entire body quivered. A prickle of unease ran down Beth's spine. This wasn't his squirrel-chasing bark, or even his suspicious-stranger bark. This felt different. Worried. Alarmed.

"Snickers, what is it?" she asked, quickening her pace, moving off the path and toward the dock, peering around the brightly-colored paddleboat, trying to see what had captured her dog's frantic attention at the water's edge. Her boots squelched slightly in the damp grass near the shore.

Rounding the paddleboat, her eyes scanned the water near the dock pilings where Snickers stood sentinel, still barking urgently, a low whine now mixed in. At first, she saw nothing alarming – just the gentle lap of water against the weathered wood, the distorted reflection of the early morning sky, maybe a stray piece of bark or leaf floating near the edge, caught in the slight current. Then she saw it. Bobbing gently against a piling, nudged by the water's movement, was a hat. A man's hat. A sharp, stylish fedora, the color of rich maple, instantly recognizable from the day before.

Nigel Verner's signature fedora.

A cold fist clenched in Beth's stomach. Why would his hat be floating in the water? Had it blown off in a nonexistent wind? Had he dropped it while admiring the view? The sight felt jarringly wrong, out of place in the tranquil morning scene. Snickers whined again, a low, distressed sound, nudging Beth's leg insistently as if urging her to understand, to look closer.

Her gaze lifted almost involuntarily from the floating hat, scanning the water just beyond it, peering into the slightly murky depths near the dock, her heart beginning to hammer against her ribs.

Seeing him.

Submerged just beneath the surface, distorted slightly by the water's movement like a reflection in flawed glass, was a figure. Pale face turned upward toward the hazy sky, sandy hair waving like dark seaweed in the gentle current, limbs adrift in a horrifyingly passive way. Dark trousers, white shirt ballooning slightly around him.

Beth gasped, a sharp, ragged intake of breath, stumbling back a step as if physically struck, her hand flying to her mouth. The world seemed to tilt and fade at the edges, the peaceful morning sounds – the lapping water, the distant loon, Snickers' frantic barks – dissolving into a roaring in her ears.

He wasn't moving. His eyes were partially open, gazing at nothing. He looked ... wrong. Terribly, irrevocably wrong. Slack. Still.

Too still.

The crisp air suddenly felt icy cold against her skin, raising goosebumps despite the emerging sun.

Nigel Verner, the arrogant critic, the man who had swept through the expo like minor royalty just yesterday, leaving a trail of pronouncements and bruised egos in his wake, was floating dead in the water.

THREE

The temporary incident room Manny Piccott had set up in a small, unused conference room at the Cedar Shore Inn felt sterile and cold, despite the lukewarm tea Manny had managed to procure. Outside the window, the cheerful blue and white bunting of the Culinary Expo flapped incongruously near the yellow police tape cordoning off the dock. The contrast felt jarring.

Beth shivered, pulling her cardigan tighter, the image of Nigel Verner's pale, submerged face still vivid behind her eyes. Penny sat beside her, unusually quiet, her usual bright energy subdued by the morning's grim discovery.

Snickers, sensing the tension, lay pressed against Beth's ankles, emitting low, unhappy sighs.

The door swung open, and Chief Galloway entered. He was a large man, and he filled the space with an air of harried importance, his uniform straining across his generous midsection, his face flushed. He'd climbed the ranks in Windy Hollow more through longevity and town connections than any notable detective skill, and he viewed anything that disturbed the town's placid surface – especially anything requiring actual investigation – as a personal affront. He nodded curtly at Beth and Penny, his gaze settling impatiently on Manny.

"Right, Piccott," Galloway huffed, pulling out a chair and sitting down heavily. "Talked to the innkeeper, Baynard. Verner apparently had a few too many glasses of that fancy chardonnay last night, held court by the wine station being obnoxious as usual. Simple explanation: stumbled down to the lake for air, lost his footing on the dock, hit his head, fell in. Tragic accident. End of story. Let's get this scene cleared up before the lunchtime expo crowd arrives. Don't want yellow tape ruining the ambiance, bad for tourism." He waved a dismissive hand, clearly eager to sweep the whole unpleasantness under the rug.

Manny met the chief's gaze steadily. "Sir, the preliminary report from the ME came in just before you arrived. There are marks on Mr. Verner's neck. Consistent with pressure applied before he entered the water. And water in the lungs confirms drowning, but the head trauma likely occurred dockside, not from a simple fall into the lake."

Galloway's face purpled slightly. "Marks? Could be anything. Caught his ascot on a piling. Tripped over a rope. The dock's probably slippery down there. Don't go looking for zebras, Piccott. It's a horse. Accidental death. Plain and simple."

"But Chief," Beth interjected softly, unable to stay silent, "Mr. Verner wasn't just unlikeable, he was deliberately cruel. He made a scene at my booth yesterday, knocked over pastries ... he seemed to enjoy upsetting people. Couldn't someone have finally snapped?"

Galloway turned his gaze on her, his expression condescending. "Ms. Sanders, with all due respect, leave the police work to us. Hurt feelings over a tart don't usually lead to murder. People like Verner make enemies, yes, but that doesn't mean they get pushed off docks. He likely slipped. Rich food, too much wine ..."

"Actually," Penny added, finding her voice, "the dock wasn't particularly slippery when Beth and I walked down there earlier. And those marks Manny mentioned ... they sound specific. Not like a random fall."

Galloway puffed out his cheeks, looking pointedly at Manny as if to say, "See what you've started?" He addressed Penny directly, his tone patronizing. "Ms. Whittaker, I appreciate your ... observations. But crime scenes aren't like the mysteries in your bookstore. Real life is usually much simpler. A man drinks too much, he falls, he drowns. Happens." He looked back at Manny. "Unless you have concrete evidence otherwise, Piccott, we proceed with accidental death." Manny shifted uncomfortably, avoiding Beth and Penny's eyes, a slight flush creeping up his neck.

"With respect, Chief," Manny persisted calmly, "the ME feels strongly the evidence points away from a simple accident. We need to treat this as suspicious, at least until we can rule out foul play."

Galloway grumbled, running a hand over his thinning hair. He hated complications, especially ones involving wealthy expo visitors that could draw unwanted press attention. "Fine, fine. Suspicious. But keep it quiet. And find an explanation, fast. Any witnesses? Anyone see him last night?"

"Ms. Baynard saw him arguing with someone near the boathouse path yesterday afternoon, but couldn't see who it was," Manny reported. "And Ms. Sanders found the body this morning."

Galloway grunted, barely glancing at Beth. "Right. Any obvious enemies here? Apart from everyone he ever reviewed?" He clearly wasn't taking the possibility seriously. "Who are the big players Verner might have tangled with yesterday? Anyone with money or influence?"

Manny considered. Verner's world revolved around high-stakes culinary ventures. "Julian Croft, the investor, is here scouting talent. Verner's reviews directly impact investments like his. It's logical to start there, establish his timeline."

Galloway nodded, seeming slightly mollified by the mention of a wealthy suspect. "Right. Croft. Sounds promising. Talk to him." Manny picked up the internal phone. "Let's see what Mr. Croft has to say."

Julian Croft arrived looking impeccable, radiating cool confidence despite the circumstances. He offered condolences with practiced smoothness, lamenting the loss of Verner's "unique critical voice." He seemed entirely unruffled.

"Mr. Croft," Manny began, "we understand you're staying at the inn for the expo?"

"Indeed. Scouting for potential investments. Some promising talent here," Croft replied, his eyes scanning the room as if assessing its potential, finding it lacking.

"Were you acquainted with Mr. Verner?"

A flicker of something – distaste? – crossed Croft's features before being smoothed away. "Acquainted, yes. We moved in similar circles, though our paths rarely crossed amicably. Nigel had ... strong opinions. Very strong."

"Did you happen to see him late last night, or perhaps early this morning?" Manny asked.

"Certainly not," Croft stated firmly. "As I believe I mentioned to Ms. Baynard when she inquired earlier, I hosted a late dinner for potential investors in my suite. It concluded shortly before midnight, and I retired. My valet attended me." He sounded utterly convincing, maybe a little too rehearsed.

Manny thanked him. Croft gave a polite, tight smile and departed, leaving the scent of expensive cologne lingering in the sterile room.

"Well?" Galloway demanded as the door closed. "Seems straightforward enough. Man's got an alibi. Solid. Valet confirmed." He looked triumphant. "See, Piccott? Simple."

"A valet-provided alibi," Manny murmured thoughtfully, looking unconvinced.

"What's that supposed to mean?" Galloway snapped. "Staff are reliable witnesses. Look, Piccott, don't overthink this. Keep it simple. Maybe Verner argued with one of those temperamental chefs, maybe he just fell. Either way, I want minimal fuss." He heaved himself out of the chair. "I'm heading back to the station. You handle the scene release. And keep me updated – brief updates." He bustled out, leaving Manny, Beth, and Penny in the quiet room.

Beth looked at Manny, shaking her head slightly. "He seemed almost too calm, didn't he? Croft?"

Penny nodded agreement. "Like he was performing. Polished. And did you notice how he never quite met your eye, Manny?"

Manny sighed, rubbing his temples. "Galloway wants it simple. He wants it closed. But you're right, it feels ... off. Croft had that air about him, like he knew more than he was saying." He stood up. "I need to do one final sweep of the dock area before the ME's team finishes and we release the scene completely. Sometimes you find things once the initial chaos settles." He looked at Beth and Penny. "You two head home, get some rest. I appreciate you waiting. I'll be in touch."

Beth and Penny nodded, gathering their things, the adrenaline fading, leaving only exhaustion and a deep sense of unease. As they walked out, they saw Manny head back toward the lakefront, his figure determined as he scanned the ground near the dock where Nigel Verner's life had so abruptly ended.

He moved slowly, methodically, his eyes sweeping the damp grass and the weathered wood of the pilings. Just as he reached the spot where the yellow tape met the edge of the lawn, his gaze caught a faint glint half-hidden in the matted grass near a piling, pressed slightly into the damp earth as if stepped on during a scuffle. He crouched down. Partially obscured by mud and grass blades lay a sleek, dark, metallic object. Distinctive calligraphy adorned its body.

It was a tasting fork, Nigel Verner's tasting fork. In the matted grass, where a struggle could have occurred.

It seemed this was no simple fall.

FOUR

Back in the makeshift incident room at the Cedar Shore Inn – a space that smelled faintly of stale coffee and disinfectant – Manny Piccott carefully laid Nigel Verner's silver tasting fork on a clean evidence sheet under the harsh glare of a desk lamp. He leaned closer, examining the tines with meticulous care. Just as he'd noted by the dockside, there were no visible traces of blood, which supported the Medical Examiner's initial suspicion of asphyxiation before Verner hit the water.

What caught his attention again were the few dark, thread-like fibers snagged tightly around the ornate base of the handle, near where Verner's initials, *NV*, were elegantly scripted.

He gently teased one loose with tweezers, holding it up to the light. It wasn't silk from Verner's ascot, nor fine wool from his expensive suit. It looked coarser, more utilitarian – a dark grey or black, possibly a cotton blend, maybe even canvas or some kind of webbing. It felt out of place, snagged on such an elegant, personal item. He rolled the fiber between his gloved fingers. It had a rough texture.

The door opened abruptly, and Chief Galloway entered, looking impatient and slightly self-satisfied. "Anything new, Piccott? Are we still looking at a clumsy fall by a drunk critic?"

Manny held up the evidence bag containing the fork. "Found this in the matted grass near the piling, Chief. Verner's signature tasting fork. Looks like it was dropped during a struggle." He pointed to the fibers with the tweezers. "And these were snagged at the base of the handle. Don't look like they came from Verner's clothing."

Galloway peered at the bag, squinting. "A fork? So what? The man probably carried it everywhere, tasting things. Dropped it when he slipped." He waved a dismissive hand at the fibers. "Pocket lint! Fluff! Means nothing. Honestly, Piccott, you're reaching.

Any signs of a real fight? Bruises? Torn clothes? Anything substantial?"

"The ME didn't note significant bruising in the initial overview," Manny admitted, "but the marks on the neck—"

"Marks that could be anything!" Galloway interrupted, his voice rising. "A rope burn from the dock, catching his collar on a splinter ... Look, unless you find something concrete, this is accidental death. Now, I heard the divers are going in to do a final sweep under the dock, standard procedure. Let me know if they find his wallet; otherwise, wrap this up." His disinterest in subtle clues that complicated his preferred narrative was obvious. Irritated by Manny's persistence and refusal to accept the easy answer, he turned to leave.

Manny watched him go, frustration tightening his jaw. He knew Galloway wanted this closed, wanted the potential scandal contained, especially with the expo bringing attention to the area. But the fork, the fibers, the matted grass, the ME's initial concerns about the neck marks ... it didn't feel like an accident. He carefully sealed the bag containing the fibers, marking it for the lab. Lint or not, it needed analysis.

Galloway could bluster all he wanted, but Manny wouldn't close the file until he was satisfied.

Beth and Penny pushed through the door of Sweets and Treats, the familiar chime a welcome sound after the cold sterility of the inn's conference room and the grimness of the morning. The bakery was warm, filled with the comforting aroma of yeast and sugar, a stark contrast to the scent of lake water and fear that clung to Beth's memory. Sophie looked up from arranging scones on a platter, her expression immediately shifting from concentration to concern as she took in their pale faces.

"Everything okay?" Sophie asked quietly, wiping her hands on her apron. "The expo gossip mill is working over-time. People are saying all sorts ... mostly that Mr. Verner finally choked on his own spite."

"It's ... not good, Soph," Beth admitted, forcing a weary smile as she untied her scarf. "Nigel Verner. He's dead. Found him by the dock this morning."

Sophie gasped, her eyes widening, dropping a scone back onto the tray with a soft thud. "Mr. Verner? Dead? But ... how?"

"They don't know yet," Penny jumped in, shedding her coat and making a beeline for the coffeepot. "Police are calling it 'suspicious,' which is cop-speak for 'we haven't got a clue but it definitely wasn't natural causes.' Although Chief Galloway seems determined to call it an accident before sundown."

She poured herself a generous mug. "Anyone else need

caffeine? My brain feels like it's been through a tumble dryer trying to process this."

Beth tied on a fresh apron, the familiar weight settling her nerves slightly. "We should probably open up properly. The afternoon crowd will be here soon, especially with the expo paused for the investigation." Work felt like the only anchor in a suddenly turbulent sea. Keeping busy was the only way to stop replaying the image of Verner's body in the water.

As Beth and Sophie prepped the counter, laying out croissants and muffins, the first of the regulars began to trickle in, drawn perhaps by the need for comfort food or, more likely, the irresistible pull of local drama.

Mrs. Higgins, owner of the yarn shop, peered over her spectacles, her knitting needles momentarily still. "Beth, dear, heard the dreadful news. Such a shock! Right here during the expo. Terrible for the town's image."

She lowered her voice conspiratorially, leaning over a tray of cinnamon rolls. "Always thought there was something shifty about that critic fellow, mind you. Too slick. Never trust a man with shoes that shiny."

Mr. Abernathy from the hardware store added his two cents while ordering a bear claw, his voice booming slightly in the suddenly quiet shop. "Mark my words, it was one of those fancy chefs. Temperamental lot. Probably argued over a soufflé or some such nonsense. Things get heated in kitchens, you know. Seen it myself back in the Army."

Beth exchanged a weary look with Penny. The speculation was running wild already.

Mr. Abernathy leaned closer, his voice dropping to a conspiratorial whisper. "I heard Chef Dubois yelling 'He got what he deserved!' He's an angry man."

Then Greta Moffat bustled in, clutching a vase she

presumably needed refilling for the inn. "Beth, Penny, you poor dears! Right in the thick of it again!" Greta thrived on local happenings, her eyes bright with morbid curiosity mixed with genuine concern.

"When I was there yesterday dropping off my center-pieces, I saw that chef – Dubois, isn't it? – having quite the set-to with Isla Baynard near the lakeside path. Very heated! Dubois was waving his arms toward the lake, seemed quite distraught about something. Pointing right at the water, he was! And then Verner upsetting someone else about their dish yesterday. Really."

Beth's interest sharpened, pushing aside her fatigue. Chef Dubois? Arguing with Isla? About what? "Really, Greta?" Beth asked, trying to keep her voice casual as she bagged Mr. Abernathy's pastry. "What were they saying? Did you hear?"

"Couldn't hear properly, dear," Greta admitted, slightly deflated but quickly recovering her dramatic flair. "Too far away. But Dubois looked absolutely furious, like thunder, and Isla seemed quite flustered, smoothing her skirt like she does when she's rattled. Made me wonder, you know? Especially now ..." She let the implication hang in the air, heavy with unspoken suspicion, paid for her usual morning scone, and bustled out, leaving Beth and Penny thoughtful. An argument near the lake? It felt significant, another tangled thread.

"Dubois?" Penny murmured, once Greta was out of earshot. "He definitely seems hotheaded. But arguing with Isla by the lake the day before ... the timing is certainly interesting."

"Maybe it was just about expo arrangements?" Beth suggested, though doubt lingered. "Isla looked stressed yesterday."

"Possibly," Penny conceded, "but it's another name to add to the list of people unhappy with Verner or potentially near the scene."

Just as the main lunch rush began, with Sophie expertly handling a sudden influx of customers seeking solace in sugar, Beth's private line buzzed in the back office. She picked it up quickly. It was Manny. His voice was low, stripped of its usual easygoing tone, tight with urgency.

"Beth, the full ME report just landed. Galloway hasn't seen it yet." He paused, and Beth held her breath. "Verner's hyoid bone is fractured. Clean break. The ME confirms it's consistent with manual strangulation. Minimal water in the lungs. He was dead, or close to it, before he ever hit the lake surface. There's no doubt now. This was murder."

Beth sank onto the office stool, the receiver cold against her ear. Murder. Strangulation. Not a fall, not an accident. Someone had deliberately, expertly, killed Nigel Verner. She relayed the stark news to Penny in a hushed voice when she returned to the counter. Penny's face went pale. The casual gossip and speculation suddenly felt chillingly real.

Two questions floated to the surface in her mind as she worked to process this information:

Who could have despised him that much to strangle him?

And who had the expertise to make it look, almost, like an accident?

FIVE

The confirmation of murder hung heavy in the air of the Sweets and Treats back office, thick and cloying like burnt sugar. Beth stared at the phone Manny had just hung up, the words "manual strangulation" echoing in the sudden quiet. Nigel Verner hadn't just fallen in and drowned.

He had been killed, deliberately, and with chilling efficiency.

The image of the elegant tasting fork, found incongruously in the damp, matted grass, flashed in her mind, those dark, snagged fibers hinting at a final, desperate struggle. Penny paced the small space, a caged tiger in a floral scarf, her usual vibrant energy replaced with a tense restlessness.

"Strangled," Penny repeated, the word sharp in the small room. She pushed a hand through her auburn curls, making them stand on end. "Galloway can't possibly call that an accident at this point."

She stopped pacing abruptly and looked at Beth, her eyes narrowed in thought. "So, if it wasn't a clumsy fall, and likely not Croft despite Galloway's eagerness ... who was mad enough, and maybe strong enough, to actually do that to Verner?"

"Everyone Verner ever insulted?" Beth suggested grimly, sinking onto a flour-dusted stool and pulling Snickers closer for comfort. He rested his heavy head on her knee, sensing her distress. "Which, based on yesterday, is practically the entire expo."

She thought back to the scene at the inn, the simmering resentments barely concealed beneath starched chef whites and polite smiles. "Chef Dubois looked fit to be tied after Verner dismissed his flambé without even tasting it. He practically vibrated with fury."

"And Chef Rossi was near the lake path yesterday afternoon, according to Greta," Penny added, recalling the gossip from the bakery earlier. "Having that 'heated set-to' with Isla. Maybe she wasn't just arguing about room views or wilting hydrangeas."

"Or maybe Rossi argued with Verner himself," Beth mused, stroking Snickers' soft ears. "Isla couldn't see who Verner was arguing with, remember? Just that it was loud and angry." The timeline felt tight, confusing.

They looked at each other, the same thought forming. While Galloway and the official investigation were likely doubling down on Julian Croft, thanks to the discovery of the pen, it felt wrong. Too neat. Too convenient. The fiery French chef, with his known temper and public disdain for Verner, seemed like a much more volatile, and therefore plausible, starting point for their own inquiries.

"Right," Beth said, standing up, a new resolve firming her shoulders despite the tremor of fear the ME's report had sent through her. Verner hadn't just died; he'd been murdered. And the killer was still out there, mingling with the expo attendees. "Poor Manny has to navigate the chief's tunnel vision and Croft's smooth denials. Let's go talk to Chef Dubois again. See if his poker alibi holds up under closer scrutiny now that we know it's murder."

Penny grinned, her usual spark returning, though her eyes remained serious. "Operation Temperamental Chef is a go. Lead the way, partner. Snickers," she called to the corgi who was now alert, tail thumping softly against the floor, "duty calls! We need your expert nose for clues ... and possibly dropped canapés." Snickers scrambled to his feet, instantly ready for action, or, at least, snacks.

Navigating the expo floor again felt different now, the cheerful buzz overlaid with a sinister undertone. Every interaction seemed potentially suspect, every smile possibly masking resentment. Beth clutched Snickers' leash tightly as they approached Chef Antoine Dubois's station.

Even from a distance, they could feel the intense heat radiating from his corner of the ballroom, smelling the sharp tang of burning sugar and orange liqueur. Dubois, a compact man with intense dark eyes and a perpetually furrowed brow emphasized by his tall toque blanche, was in the midst of a dramatic demonstration, wielding a copper pan like a weapon.

With a flourish that sent droplets of flaming liquid dangerously close to the tablecloth, he ignited the contents, sending a whoosh of orange flame shooting toward the ceiling, eliciting gasps and slightly nervous applause from the small crowd gathered.

"Showman," Penny muttered under her breath as they waited for a lull, strategically positioning themselves near the edge of the crowd but within clear view. "Or pyromaniac."

When the flames subsided and the applause died down, Beth stepped forward cautiously, Penny close behind.

"Chef Dubois? Excuse me, could we have a quick word? It's important."

Dubois turned, wiping his brow with the back of his hand, his expression impatient, clearly annoyed at the interruption. "Oui? You wish to sample the crêpes Suzette? Be quick, I am very busy. These people," he gestured to the audience, "they appreciate true artistry."

"Actually, Chef," Beth began, trying to keep her voice calm and nonaccusatory, "we wanted to ask about Mr. Verner again. The police now believe his death wasn't an accident. He was murdered." She watched his face closely for a reaction.

Dubois's eyes widened slightly, but his expression quickly hardened. He shrugged, a Gallic gesture of indifference that didn't quite ring true. "Murdered? Eh bien. Perhaps someone finally tired of his poisonous tongue. It is not surprising. As I told you, I was not his biggest fan."

"Indeed," Penny interjected smoothly. "You mentioned he destroyed your cousin's bistro in Lyon with one review. Called his coq au vin 'provincial sludge,' I believe you said?"

Dubois slammed the copper pan down on the burner again, making Beth and several onlookers jump. "Oui! That imbécile! Jean-Pierre poured his heart, his soul, his inheritance into that bistro! And Verner crushed him like a snail under foot! Provincial sludge! Bah! Jean-Pierre never recovered. He lost everything." Dubois's face was flushed, his fists clenched. "Verner deserved far worse than falling off some dock! He deserved to be slowly poached in his own arrogance!"

"A strong sentiment, Chef," Beth said quietly. "Strong enough to act on, perhaps? Where exactly were you last night? Around, say, ten p.m. onward?"

Dubois waved a dismissive hand, though his agitation

was palpable. He gestured toward a group of chefs lingering near Chef Rossi's booth. "I told you! I was playing poker. A friendly game. Ask them. Bellwether, Rossi ... though Bellwether," he added with a sneer, "he folded early, claiming 'inspiration' struck. Bah! More likely indigestion from his own over-sauced quail. That man has the constitution of a nervous rabbit."

He lowered his voice slightly, leaning toward them conspiratorially. "If you seek a killer, mademoiselles, look to the one whose career Verner almost ended before it began. Bellwether still trembles like an unset panna cotta when Verner's name is mentioned. Voilà."

He turned back to his crêpes with an air of finality, clearly dismissing them.

Beth and Penny exchanged a frustrated glance. Dubois was fiery, practically radiating motive, but his poker alibi, even with Bellwether leaving early, seemed plausible enough, involving multiple potential witnesses. It felt like another dead end. As they turned to leave, Snickers, perhaps bored with the lack of dropped food or sensing the tension, suddenly tugged hard on his leash. He darted under the edge of Dubois's draped prep table, sniffing intently at something near a small metal waste bin tucked discreetly out of sight amongst boxes of supplies.

"Snickers, heel!" Beth commanded, pulling gently on the leash, embarrassed by the interruption.

But Snickers refused to budge, instead pawing insistently at a small, crumpled piece of paper lying half-hidden amongst some discarded orange peels and sugar wrappers near the bin. It looked like ordinary trash, but Snickers nudged it with his nose toward Penny, letting out a low growl, his usual cheerful demeanor replaced by focused intensity.

"What have you got there, boy?" Penny crouched down, cautiously reaching under the table, mindful of Dubois's glare. She emerged holding the paper gingerly between her thumb and forefinger. It was charred around the edges, crumpled tightly as if someone had tried to burn it and then hastily discarded it.

Unfolding it carefully, avoiding the burnt sections, they saw fragments of typed words. Parts were missing, consumed by the flame, but enough remained to be chillingly clear: '...igel Verner... final warning ... pay what is owed ... or face the consequences ...'

Beth's breath caught. She looked up sharply at Dubois, who was watching them now, his face suddenly pale beneath his chef's hat, his earlier bravado evaporating like burnt-off brandy. He took an involuntary step back.

"What is this, Chef?" Beth asked, her voice low and steady, holding up the damning fragment. "A final warning? Pay what is owed? It sounds rather threatening."

Dubois stared at the paper as if it were a viper about to strike, his eyes wide with panic. He swallowed hard, his Adam's apple bobbing. "Non! It is not mine! I know nothing of this! It is absurd!"

He pointed a shaking finger across the ballroom toward Bellwether's elegant booth.

"It must be him! Bellwether! He tries to frame me! He hates me, you know! Always jealous of my technique! This is his doing! He planted it!" His voice rose, attracting curious glances from nearby attendees.

SIX

Leaving Chef Dubois fuming amidst the lingering scent of burnt sugar and indignation, Beth and Penny navigated the bustling expo floor toward Chef Marcus Bellwether's station. The Frenchman's accusations, flung like stray drops of flaming liqueur, hung in the air between them.

"Bellwether planted the note? Seriously?" Penny scoffed, adjusting her scarf. "Dubois is just deflecting. Though," she conceded, "Bellwether certainly had reason to despise Verner. That review Dubois mentioned ... nearly ending his career? That kind of wound festers."

Compared to Dubois's fiery chaos, Bellwether's setup was an oasis of calm elegance. Crisp white linens, gleaming copper pots arranged with geometric precision, and towering displays of perfectly glazed fruit tarts and intricate pastries spoke of meticulous control and high-end success.

Bellwether himself, tall and silver-haired with laugh lines crinkling around his eyes, greeted approaching guests with the practiced charm of a seasoned restaurateur, offering samples of a delicate elderflower panna cotta on tiny silver spoons. He looked every inch the successful, established chef, a world away from the struggling newcomer Verner had once tried to crush.

"Ah, Ms. Sanders, Ms. Whittaker," he said smoothly as they approached, his smile encompassing them both, though Beth thought she detected a flicker of wariness in his eyes. "Come to sample the delights? Or perhaps seeking refuge from Chef Dubois's ... pyrotechnics?" He chuckled softly, a low, cultured sound. "Antoine does get rather carried away, doesn't he? Passionate, I suppose one calls it."

"His passion nearly set fire to his tablecloth," Penny remarked dryly, accepting a small spoon of panna cotta. She savored it for a moment. "Delicious, Chef. Truly."

"Thank you. Simplicity and quality ingredients, that's the key," Bellwether replied. Penny noted a fleeting nervousness, a subtle tremor just beneath his polished surface as his gaze darted briefly toward the main entrance, then back.

"Chef Bellwether," Beth began, deciding a direct approach was best, "we understand the police are now treating Mr. Verner's death as murder."

Bellwether's smile tightened almost imperceptibly. He carefully wiped the edge of a pristine display plate with a folded white cloth. "Yes, a dreadful business. Shocking. Nigel could be difficult, of course, difficult for many people ... but murder ... it's unthinkable in a place like this."

"You knew him well?" Penny asked, her tone light but her eyes sharp.

"Our paths crossed over the years," Bellwether admitted, his gaze flickering away again toward a display of spun sugar. "He reviewed my first restaurant venture. Quite harshly, as it happens." He attempted another chuckle, but it sounded strained, brittle. "Nearly put me out of business before I'd even started. Water under the bridge now, of course. One learns, one adapts." He meticulously rearranged a display of miniature lavender cheesecakes, his grip tight on the serving tongs.

Penny watched his hands, noticing the faint, faded edge of a dark blue tattoo peeking out from under the starched white cuff of his chef's jacket – something intricate, almost tribal, a stark contrast to his current refined image. It hinted at a different life, a past perhaps less polished than his present.

Had Penny overheard some vague kitchen gossip once about Bellwether having completely "reinvented himself" after some unspecified trouble years ago? She made a mental note to research him later.

"That review must have been devastating at the time," Beth pressed gently. "Chef Dubois seemed to think you still felt strongly about it."

Bellwether stiffened visibly, placing the tongs down with a soft, deliberate click. "Antoine exaggerates. And gossips." His voice lost its earlier warmth, becoming clipped and defensive. "Yes, it was difficult. Nigel's words carried weight, disproportionate weight. But I rebuilt. Moved on. Started over."

He made a vague gesture around his elegant booth, though the gesture lacked conviction. "Success is the best revenge, wouldn't you agree?" There was a hardness in his eyes now, a glimpse of steel beneath the charm.

"Where were you the night before last, Chef?" Beth asked, keeping her voice level. "After you left the poker game?"

Bellwether frowned, finally meeting her gaze, though his eyes were cold. "Poker game? Oh, yes. Dubois's little gathering. I left early, as Antoine likely told you with great relish. Inspiration struck for a new dessert concept – a deconstructed Black Forest gateau. I went back to my room at the inn, sketched out some ideas. Worked quite late, actually."

"Alone?" Penny queried, leaning forward slightly.

"Naturally," Bellwether snapped, his composure fraying. "Creativity requires solitude. Unlike some chefs who require an audience for their theatrics." He picked up his polishing cloth again, rubbing furiously at an already gleaming copper bowl.

"Look, I barely knew Verner in recent years. Our paths diverged significantly. Dubois, on the other hand ... their feud was legendary. And quite recent. Did he show you that ridiculous note he claims I planted?"

He scoffed, a harsh, barking sound. "As if I'd be so clumsy! If anyone planted anything, it was Antoine, trying to stir up trouble, deflect from his own questionable dealings."

Just as Bellwether paused for breath, Isla Baynard hurried past his booth, clipboard clutched tightly, her expression harried. Beth quickly stepped out, intercepting her. "Isla, excuse me, just a moment?"

Isla stopped, tapping her pen impatiently against the clipboard. "Yes, Beth? It's rather hectic. We're trying to manage the schedule changes now that ... well, now that Mr. Verner won't be giving his keynote."

"I understand, I'm so sorry to bother you. It's just, you mentioned seeing Mr. Verner arguing with someone near the boathouse path the afternoon before ... before he was found. Are you absolutely sure you couldn't see who it was? Or overhear anything at all?"

Isla frowned in concentration, tucking a stray blonde hair behind her ear, her gaze distant for a moment. "No, I'm afraid not. I was dealing with that catering delivery issue near the terrace, quite some distance away. I just registered raised voices, angry gestures. Verner was certainly agitated, pacing back and forth, jabbing his finger. The other person ... honestly, their back was mostly toward me, and they were partly obscured by the big willow tree down there. I was focused on trying to sort out why we'd received three crates of Belgian endive instead of artichoke hearts."

She sighed, the stress evident in the lines around her eyes. "I wish I could be more help. It's dreadful, this whole affair. A murder investigation during our biggest event of the year ..." She gave a brief, apologetic smile and hurried off toward the main stage, already consulting her clipboard.

Beth rejoined Penny, who raised an eyebrow hopefully. "No luck?"

"No. Just confirmation there was an argument, but still no idea who with." Beth felt a familiar sense of frustration. Every lead seemed promising initially, only to dissolve into ambiguity or deflection. Bellwether was defensive and hiding something – perhaps just an old embarrassment, perhaps more. Dubois was volatile and had motive.

Her phone vibrated in her apron pocket. Seeing Manny's name flash on the small screen, she answered quickly, stepping slightly away from Bellwether's booth, turning her back for privacy. "Manny? Any news?"

"Beth, we found Nigel's tasting fork. It was in nearby grass, somewhat beat down, possibly in a scuffle. There were some common nylon or canvas fibers in the tines, but nothing obvious from what he was wearing."

Beth processed this, trying to imagine if maybe he had a small sachet for the fork. None that she ever saw. "So possibly lost in a fight?"

"Yes, that was my thinking as well. There was something else from the ME." Manny's voice was low, serious, cutting through the background hum of the expo. "While searching for a source of the blend fibers, they did a thorough check of Verner's clothing. They found another type of fiber, different from the ones on the fork."

"Different how?" Beth asked, her pulse quickening. Another clue?

"This one was caught right under the back collar of his shirt, near the neck, almost hidden in the seam. It's finer than the fork fibers, almost iridescent, a greenish-gold color. Definitely not cotton or canvas. The lab confirms it's plant-based, but from something non-native. Exotic. Definitely not from any plant known to grow wild around Windy Hollow or the Cedar Shore grounds."

Beth relayed the information quickly to Penny. The fork with the nylon fibers, and a different fiber in the collar. Plant-based. Exotic.

"Could it be from Bellwether's orchid delivery?" Penny whispered excitedly. "Or maybe Rossi? Or Dubois? Don't chefs use all sorts of weird leaves and petals for garnish these days? Things imported from who-knows-where?"

Beth nodded slowly, the possibilities swirling. "Saffron threads, rare barks, edible flowers ... Bellwether himself mentioned sourcing unique elements."

The new clue, instead of narrowing the field, seemed to throw suspicion back onto the chefs themselves, onto their very craft. It was another layer of complexity, making the path to the truth feel even more obscured.

SEVEN

The news of the second, more unusual fiber found on Nigel Verner's collar – fine, iridescent, and plant-based – sent a fresh wave of determination through Beth, Penny, and Sophie. Manny, armed with this new piece of forensic evidence, had managed to convince a still-grumbling Chief Galloway that further investigation into the expo attendees was warranted.

The next morning, the back room of Sweets and Treats, usually redolent with the scent of cinnamon and rising dough, was transformed into an impromptu research hub. Sophie, her own laptop open in front of her, typed furiously, her brow furrowed in concentration as she navigated online botanical databases.

Penny, meanwhile, had her own formidable research tool ready. Beside a stack of horticultural encyclopedias from her bookstore, sat her prized possession: a surprisingly powerful, custom-modified laptop running COMP-AI. COMP-AI wasn't your average search engine.

Penny, a tech enthusiast with a penchant for digital deep-dives, had acquired and continuously upgraded the

AI-driven software over the years. It was designed to sift through vast amounts of data – from obscure academic papers and archived forums to de-indexed websites and specialized trade publications – identifying patterns and connections that would elude standard searches.

It was, as Penny often quipped, "like having a team of obsessive research librarians living in a very sleek box, fueled by caffeine and algorithms."

Beth, an old school paper and pen writer, tried to organize their thoughts, while Snickers lay under the table, occasionally thumping his tail in what Beth hoped was investigative enthusiasm rather than just a dream about dropped cookies. Manny had called earlier, giving them the lab's initial analysis: the fiber was from a species of Tillandsia, commonly known as air plants, specifically a variety with fine, silvery- green, almost glittery trichomes – the tiny hair-like structures that gave it the iridescent quality. Many varieties were native to South and Central America, but some were cultivated as ornamentals worldwide.

"Tillandsia usneoides – Spanish Moss – that's a common one," Penny mused, tapping a picture in one of her encyclopedias, while simultaneously feeding keywords into COMP-AI. The AI's interface glowed with rapidly scrolling lines of text and complex diagrams. "But the lab said this was finer, more ... metallic looking. COMP-AI is flagging several rarer cultivars known for that sheen – Tillandsia argentea, funckiana, some of the more obscure hybrids. These aren't your grandma's houseplants."

"And definitely not something you'd find growing wild around Windy Hollow," Beth added, jotting down the names. "Manny said the lab was emphatic about that. It's an indoor ornamental, or something used in very specific landscaping."

Sophie looked up from her laptop. "Okay, I've cross-referenced Tillandsia varieties with lists of plants used in high-end floral design and interior landscaping for events. Some of the rarer ones, especially those with that silvery sheen, are prized for their unique texture in avant-garde arrangements or as accents in terrariums and living walls." She scrolled through a page of images – delicate, other-worldly plants that looked more like alien sculptures than something from Earth. "They're not your every day garden center fare, that's for sure. You'd have to source them from a specialist supplier."

"First things first," Beth said, tapping her pen. "We need to rule out the obvious. Could it have come from the Cedar Shore Inn itself? Isla Baynard is meticulous about the inn's appearance. Maybe she has some exotic plants in the lobby or guest rooms?"

Penny consulted her phone. "Already on it. I texted Isla earlier, pretending to admire the 'unique botanical touches' at the expo and asking if she used any air plants in her decor. She just replied." Penny read from her screen: "'Lovely of you to notice, Penny, but no Tillandsia here. Our florist focuses on more traditional, robust arrangements suitable for a lakeside inn. Less ... spiky.' So, that's a no on the inn's general landscaping or floral displays."

"Okay," Beth said, drawing a line through 'Inn Land-scaping' on her pad. "What about direct floral deliveries to Nigel Verner's room? Or to any of the chefs who might have been near him?"

"Manny's looking into official expo floral orders," Sophie offered, "but he said it might take time to get the full list from all the vendors and cross-reference with Verner's known associates or room deliveries. COMP-AI might be faster on that, Penny, if you can access supplier databases or event florist networks."

"Way ahead of you, Soph," Penny said, her fingers flying across her keyboard. "COMP-AI is currently cross-referencing known expo floral suppliers with Tillandsia specialists. But a direct approach with Isla might give us a specific name faster." She stood up. "Time for another friendly chat with our favorite stressed-out innkeeper.

Coming, Beth?"

Isla Baynard, when they found her in the inn's bustling temporary office, looked even more harried than usual. Stacks of invoices teetered on her desk, and she was simultaneously on the phone and trying to direct a lost-looking staff member. She sighed when she saw Beth and Penny, but waved them toward a pair of chairs.

"Ladies, if this is about the ... unfortunate incident, Officer Piccott has all the information," Isla said, finally hanging up the phone with a weary click.

"Actually, Isla," Beth began gently, "we were wondering about floral deliveries. Specifically, any that might have gone to Mr. Verner's suite, or perhaps to any of the chefs' booths, in the last couple of days."

Isla raised a perfectly sculpted eyebrow. "Floral deliveries? What on earth for?"

"Just a small detail we're trying to clarify," Penny said vaguely. "Sometimes packaging materials ... you know. Odd fibers can turn up."

Isla sighed again, clearly unconvinced but too busy to argue. She pulled a thick binder labeled 'Expo Deliveries & Logistics' toward her. "Everything is logged. Flowers for guest rooms, booth enhancements ... let's see. Verner, Verner ..." She flipped through several pages. "Ah, here we are. Nigel Verner, Suite 301. One delivery noted for the day before yesterday – that would be the day before ... well, before." Her voice faltered slightly. "From 'Bellwether Gastronomy.' An orchid arrangement. Large. White Phalaenopsis, it says here, with 'artistic accents.'"

"Chef Bellwether sent Nigel Verner orchids?" Beth exchanged a surprised look with Penny. That seemed an unlikely gesture from a man whose career Verner had nearly torpedoed. A peace offering? Or something more calculated?

"Apparently so," Isla confirmed, tapping the entry. "Our house florist didn't handle it; it came directly from Bellwether's own supplier, noted here as 'Exotic Blooms of Asheville.'"

"Exotic Blooms of Asheville," Penny repeated, already typing the name into COMP-AI and her phone's browser simultaneously. "Got it. Thanks, Isla, you've been a great help." She paused. "Isla, one more quick thing, if you don't mind. When Mr. Verner's room was initially secured by Officer Piccott, was that orchid arrangement ... disturbed? Opened?"

Isla frowned, thinking back. "Actually, no. Officer Piccott asked me about that specifically when he was cataloging the room contents. The box from Exotic Blooms was still sealed, on the desk. Mr. Verner apparently never got around to opening it. Officer Piccott took it as evidence, of course, still sealed." Beth and Penny exchanged a significant look. Sealed. Unopened.

Back in the relative quiet of the bakery's back room, the new information settled heavily. "So, the orchid package was never opened by Verner," Beth stated, the implications clear. "Those Tillandsia fibers on his collar couldn't have come from the packing material inside that box."

"Which means," Penny said, tapping her chin thoughtfully, "if the fibers are indeed from that specific type of Tillandsia, and Exotic Blooms of Asheville is known to use it, we need to find another way Bellwether could have brought that plant material into contact with Verner, or at least into an environment where it could transfer."

Sophie, who had been quietly listening, spoke up. "Chef Bellwether's display booth ... it was very elaborate. Lots of garnishes, artistic touches. Did anyone notice if he was using any unusual plants for staging his dishes or decorating his table?"

Beth tried to recall the details of Bellwether's elegant setup. "It was all very polished. Lots of gleaming fruit, spun sugar ... but plants? I remember some greenery, but nothing that stood out as particularly exotic at the time."

"COMP-AI, pull up any available images or descriptions of Chef Marcus Bellwether's Culinary Expo booth display, focusing on decorative elements, especially botanicals," Penny commanded her laptop. The AI whirred, and, after a moment, images began to fill the screen – close-ups of Bellwether's pastries, wider shots of his station.

Penny zoomed in on one. "There! Look at this." Tucked artfully around a tiered display of miniature tarts were delicate, feathery strands of silvery-green plant material, exactly matching the encyclopedia images of the rarer Tillandsia cultivars. "He was using it as a decorative accent at his booth."

"So, the fibers could have come from his display," Beth breathed, a chill running down her spine. "Anyone who spent time near his booth, anyone handling those dishes or even brushing against the display could have picked them up." This opened up a new avenue, but also a more direct link to Bellwether himself having the fibers readily available.

Penny turned back to her COMP-AI. "Let's dig deeper into Bellwether. That name change, the reinvention ... there's more to him than just fancy pastries."

The AI hummed, its screen alive with cascading lines of data. After a few tense minutes, a soft chime indicated a significant find. Penny leaned forward, her eyes scanning the results. "Okay, here we go. Marcus Bellwether wasn't always Marcus Bellwether. He legally changed his name fifteen years ago. Before that, he was known as Marc Bell."

"Marc Bell?" Beth repeated, a knot forming in her stomach. "Does it say what he did before he became a chef?"

"Oh, it does," Penny said, her voice tight. "Marc Bell was the proprietor of a place in southern Florida called 'Bell's Botanicals.' It wasn't your average garden center.

Specialized in rare, exotic, and sometimes ... controversial plants." "Controversial how?" Sophie asked, her eyes wide.

"COMP-AI is pulling up archived local news reports and old online forum discussions," Penny explained, scrolling rapidly. "Bell's Botanicals was at the center of an informal investigation about fifteen years back. A string of unexplained illnesses, some quite severe, in an affluent nearby community. There were rumors, strong ones, that the source might have been exposure to rare toxins, possibly from plants sourced from Bell's nursery. Nothing was ever proven definitively, no charges filed. Bell sold the nursery shortly after the investigation quieted down and essentially vanished for a couple of years, only to resurface in Asheville as the reinvented Chef Marcus Bellwether."

The air in the small back office suddenly felt colder. A man with a past shrouded in rumors of poison and illness, now a celebrated chef.

"So he has a history with unusual plants, potentially

dangerous ones," Beth said, her mind racing. "What about the supplier, Exotic Blooms of Asheville? The one who provided the unopened orchid and presumably the Tillandsia for his booth display?"

Penny was already a step ahead, her fingers a blur. "Cross-referencing now ... Got it! The founder and current owner of Exotic Blooms of Asheville? A Ms. Elara Vance. And guess who her first employer was, right out of horticultural college?" Penny looked up, her expression grim. "Marc Bell. At Bell's Botanicals. Old newspaper clippings refer to her as his 'star protégé,' 'deeply knowledgeable about his specialized collection.'"

The connection was undeniable, a cold, hard link between Bellwether's hidden past and the very materials found on Nigel Verner. If the fibers didn't come from the unopened orchid package, they most likely came from the identical plants Bellwether was openly displaying.

"The specific Tillandsia," Beth emphasized, remembering Manny's report on the lab's findings. "Manny said the lab identified a particular cultivar, one known for its unusually fine, iridescent fibers." She turned to Penny. "Can COMP-AI search for any connection between Marc Bell, or Bell's Botanicals, and that specific cultivar of Tillandsia?"

Penny nodded, her brow furrowed in concentration as she fed the new parameters into the AI. The seconds stretched, filled only with the soft whir of the laptop and Snickers' occasional sigh from under the table. Then, another chime.

"Bingo," Penny whispered, her eyes fixed on the screen. She read aloud, her voice low and incredulous. "Archived newsletter from the 'South Florida Exotic Plant Society,' dated twelve years ago. There's an article here ... 'Local

Innovator Marc Bell of Bell's Botanicals Earns Acclaim for New Tillandsia Hybrid.'" She looked up at Beth and Sophie, her face pale. "It describes a new cultivar he apparently developed or perfected. And the description? 'Characterized by its exceptionally fine, almost metallic, silvery-green trichomes that create a remarkable iridescent sheen, and its surprisingly resilient fibers.'"

Beth felt a wave of nausea. It was him. Bellwether hadn't just used a plant that happened to match the fibers; he had a history, an intimate, expert knowledge of that specific, rare plant. He might have even created it. The fact that the orchid gift remained unopened now seemed less like a dead end and more like a chilling testament to Bellwether's confidence. They didn't need the orchid in Verner's room to be the source; the source material was right there at his fingertips, on public display.

She pictured Bellwether, calm and charming at his expo booth, surrounded by the very plant that could link him to a murder. The question now was, how did those fibers make their way from his display to Nigel Verner's collar at the boathouse?

Beth shuddered at the possibilities.

EIGHT

The unsettling revelations about Chef Marcus Bellwether's past – his former identity as Marc Bell, proprietor of the controversial Bell's Botanicals, and his direct link to the unique Tillandsia fiber found on Nigel Verner – had cast a long, dark shadow over the Culinary Expo.

While Chief Galloway remained stubbornly focused on accidental cause of death, Beth, Penny, and Sophie felt a growing conviction that the outwardly polished Chef Bellwether was hiding far more than just an old grudge. The question of how the fibers from his booth display ended up on Verner's collar near the boathouse was a troubling puzzle, but his potential motive needed further exploration.

"If Verner was about to skewer Bellwether with another career-ending review, especially now that he's so established, the fallout could be catastrophic for him," Beth mused the following morning. They were gathered once again in the bakery's back room, the aroma of blueberry scones doing little to dispel the tension. Snickers, sensing the mood, lay with his head on Beth's foot, emitting the occasional worried sigh.

"Exactly," Penny agreed, her fingers already flying across the COMP-AI keyboard. "A bad review for a chef at his level isn't just about hurt feelings; it's about bookings, investors, brand image ... big money. If he's financially vulnerable, that motive gets a whole lot stronger." Sophie, meanwhile, was navigating a labyrinth of public records and financial news sites on her own laptop, her brow furrowed in concentration.

It didn't take long for COMP-AI to start flagging concerning data points. "Okay, got something," Penny announced, leaning closer to her screen. "Bellwether's flagship restaurant in Asheville underwent a massive, very expensive renovation about eighteen months ago. Took out some hefty business loans to finance it. We're talking seven figures." She pulled up a series of articles detailing the lavish reopening. "Looks like he was betting big on continued success and expansion."

Sophie chimed in, her voice quiet but firm. "And according to these investment forums and stock trackers, a significant portion of Bellwether's personal investment portfolio took a nosedive in the last quarter. Looks like he was heavily invested in a tech startup that went belly-up. He'd be feeling a serious pinch."

The pieces clicked together with an ominous sound. Large debts, recent significant losses ... Chef Bellwether wasn't just protecting a reputation; he may have been fighting for his financial survival. Another scathing review from a critic as influential as Nigel Verner could have been the final straw, pushing his teetering financial house into collapse. The motive wasn't just old anger; it was fresh, pressing, and potentially desperate.

The air in the bakery's back room grew heavier with each revelation. Bellwether's financial situation painted a picture of a man under immense pressure, a man whose carefully constructed empire could crumble with one more significant blow – like a devastating review from Nigel Verner. As Penny and Sophie delved deeper into Bell-wether's financial entanglements, Penny decided to broaden her COMP-AI search.

"If he's this stressed financially, and, with his history with Verner, he might have vented somewhere online," Penny mused, her fingers already adjusting search parameters. "COMP-AI, scan high-end culinary discussion forums, private chef groups, even social media undercurrents for any anonymous or pseudonymous posts expressing extreme animosity toward critics matching Verner's profile, particularly any posts originating from or linked to the Asheville area or known associates of Bellwether."

The AI whirred, sifting through terabytes of online chatter, a digital bloodhound on a scent. After several minutes, a soft chime indicated a match. "Well, well, what have we here?" Penny murmured, leaning closer to the screen. She turned it so Beth and Sophie could see.

Displayed was a screenshot from an obscure, high-end culinary discussion forum, a members-only site known for its passionate, and often vitriolic, debates among industry professionals. The post, dated about six months prior, was written under the username "CulinarianConnoisseur72." It was a long, rambling tirade against an unnamed but easily identifiable powerful food critic – the descriptions of his methods, his specific turns of phrase, and his recent scathing reviews pointed directly and unmistakably to Nigel Verner.

The post was filled with fury, accusing the critic of wielding his power like a vindictive god, of destroying careers on a whim, of having a personal vendetta. But it was the final lines that made Beth's blood run cold: "This tyrant has gone too far. He's ruined too many good people. Someone needs to teach him a permanent lesson, a lesson he'll never forget. If no one else has the guts, mark my words, I'll find a way to serve him his just desserts, and it won't be on a silver platter."

"Permanent lesson ... just desserts ..." Sophie whispered, her face pale. "That sounds like a threat."

"COMP-AI is running a trace on 'CulinarianConnoisseur72,'" Penny said, her fingers flying. "Trying to link it to any known email addresses or IP locations associated with our suspects." A moment later, the AI beeped again. "Got it. The account was registered using a burner email, but the IP address for several of its most recent logins, including the one that made that post? It traces back to a network frequently used by ... Chef Marcus Bellwether's Asheville restaurant."

The circumstantial evidence was piling up, painting a portrait of a man pushed to the brink, both financially and emotionally.

The damning forum post, seemingly penned by Chef Bellwether himself, hung in the digital air of the bakery's back room, as tangible as the scent of yeast. "We need to show this to Manny," Beth said, her voice firm despite the unease coiling in her stomach. "And, then, we need to talk to Bellwether again. This is too direct to ignore."

Armed with a printout of the forum post and the IP trace from COMP-AI, they met Manny later that afternoon. The officer looked weary; Chief Galloway had clearly been relentless about Julian Croft and the pen. When Manny saw the forum post, however, his eyes sharpened with renewed interest. "This is ... significant," he admitted, reading the threatening words. "If we can definitively prove Bellwether wrote this, it establishes clear premeditation."

Their subsequent confrontation with Chef Bellwether was tense. They found him at his booth, meticulously polishing a silver serving dish, the picture of calm professionalism. When Beth presented him with the printout of the forum post, however, a flicker of something – fear? anger? – crossed his usually composed features. He initially scoffed, dismissing it. "This? Some online ranting? It's absurd. Anyone could have written this."

"The IP address for this post, and several others from 'CulinarianConnoisseur72,' traces back to your restaurant's network, Chef," Penny stated calmly, her gaze unwavering.

Bellwether's composure cracked slightly. He ran a hand through his silver hair, his smile becoming strained. "My network? It must have been hacked. Or perhaps a disgruntled former employee. I have many competitors, people who would love to see me discredited."

He then tried a different tack, his voice regaining some of its smooth charm. "Besides, even if I did dash off some angry words in a moment of frustration – and I'm not saying I did – online forums are hardly binding confessions. People say foolish things. It's taken entirely out of context. Surely you don't believe I'd actually act on such hyperbole?"

His denials, however plausible on the surface, felt hollow. Later, Manny relayed that Chief Galloway had become reluctantly intrigued by the mounting circumstantial case against Bellwether.

"He told me to 'get something concrete on this fancy chef, Piccott, or be ready to find a new line of work,'" Manny sighed. "So now I'm juggling two high-pressure suspects, and the Chief wants results yesterday." The pressure was mounting from all sides.

The pressure from Chief Galloway was palpable. Manny knew he needed something more definitive on Bellwether. If he couldn't find anything, it could potentially let the real killer slip away. He decided to press Bellwether again, this time specifically about his alibi for the night of Verner's murder – the night he claimed to be in his room having a late-night burst of dessert inspiration.

Manny found Bellwether supervising the breakdown of his elaborate expo booth. The chef's usual charm was wearing thin, his movements sharp and impatient. "Officer Piccott," Bellwether said, his voice tight, "I've told you, I was in my room. Working."

"And no one saw you, Chef?" Manny pressed gently. "No room service, no calls, no one you passed in the hallway?"

Bellwether hesitated, a flicker of something unreadable in his eyes. He wiped his hands meticulously on a linen towel. "As a matter of fact," he said slowly, reaching into the inner pocket of his chef's jacket, "I wasn't in my room the entire evening. I'd forgotten. Inspiration, as I said, struck for my Black Forest gâteau. I realized I was missing a rather specific, high-quality kirsch – the kind one doesn't simply find in a hotel minibar, or even in Windy Hollow, for that matter."

He produced a folded receipt from his wallet and handed it to Manny. "I drove to Portland. There's a specialty liquor store there that stocks it. As you can see by the time stamp, I made my purchase at precisely 10:47 p.m. It's nearly an hour's drive each way, especially at night."

Manny examined the receipt. It was from "The Connoisseur's Cellar" in Portland, time-stamped, as Bellwether claimed, for one bottle of expensive kirsch.

The murder was believed to have occurred sometime between 10 p.m. and midnight.

If Bellwether was in Portland at 10:47 p.m., it would

make it incredibly difficult, though perhaps not entirely impossible, for him to have been at the Cedar Shore Inn boathouse during the crucial window.

It didn't clear him completely – he could have attacked Verner before leaving for Portland, or even upon his return if the timing was tight – but it certainly complicated the narrative of him being the one to strangle Verner by the lake.

The receipt felt like a carefully produced trump card, weakening the straightforward case they were building against him, yet not quite shattering it.

Manny sighed. It was another frustrating layer of ambiguity from the enigmatic chef.

NINE

Chef Bellwether's Portland receipt, with its inconveniently timed purchase of kirsch, had thrown a partial wrench into the gears of Beth and Penny's investigation. While it didn't entirely exonerate him – the timing was tight, but not impossible for him to have been involved – it did muddy the waters considerably, forcing them to re-evaluate their other prime suspect: the volatile Chef Antoine Dubois. The image of the Frenchman's fiery outburst and the discovery of that partially burnt, threatening note near his station still loomed large in their minds.

"Bellwether's alibi is ... annoying," Penny conceded, sipping her morning coffee in the bakery's back room. The scent of freshly baked croissants, usually a comfort, did little to sweeten her mood. "It feels a bit too convenient, a bit too neat, but it's enough to make Galloway ease off him if Manny presents it."

"Which means Dubois moves back to the top of the list," Beth said, tapping a pen against her notepad. Snickers, ever attuned to their investigative huddles, looked up from his nap, his brow furrowed in a perfect imitation of deep thought.

"That note Snickers found ... 'final warning ... pay what is owed ...' It felt personal. And Dubois certainly had a personal vendetta against Verner after what happened to his cousin's bistro."

Sophie, who was meticulously dusting a tray of éclairs, paused. "The note was typed, mostly. But what about any handwritten parts? Were there any? Or any symbols, anything distinctive?"

Penny pulled up the crime scene photo of the note on her COMP-AI. "Most of it is typed, standard font. But the edges were so charred, and it was crumpled ... Wait a minute." She zoomed in on a tiny, less-burnt fragment at the very bottom corner. "There's something here ... it looks like a hastily scribbled initial or a symbol, almost like a chef's mark."

Beth leaned closer. "It's so small. Could it be anything?"

"Let's compare," Penny said, her fingers already flying. "Remember when Dubois was arguing with Bellwether about the crêpes Suzette? He grabbed a napkin and scribbled down a modified ingredient list for Bellwether to 'improve' his supposedly inferior version."

Penny had, with her usual foresight, snagged the discarded napkin. She pulled the scanned image of it onto the screen alongside the note fragment. There, on the napkin, scrawled with impatient, angular strokes, was Chef Dubois's signature flourish after a particularly scathing comment about Bellwether's lack of classic technique.

It wasn't an exact match to the tiny mark on the burnt note, but the aggressive slant, the sharp, almost angry way the lines were formed ... there was a definite, unsettling resemblance. It was a small thing, perhaps nothing, but it was enough to reignite their suspicions about the fiery Frenchman.

The possible similarity between Dubois's scribbled flourish and the mark on the burnt note was tenuous, but it was enough to send Beth and Penny back to re-examine his alibi: the infamous poker game. Dubois had been adamant that he was playing cards with several other chefs, including Chef Rossi and, for a time, Chef Bellwether, during the period Verner was likely murdered. However, Bellwether had claimed Dubois was still there when he left early to pursue his dessert inspiration.

"If Dubois did leave that poker game, and Bellwether wasn't there to see it, who would know?" Beth wondered aloud, dusting flour from her apron. "Chef Rossi was supposedly there the whole time. Maybe she'd be willing to talk, especially if she thought Dubois was trying to use her as a false alibi."

Penny, ever resourceful, had already pulled up the Culinary Expo's official participant list on COMP-AI. "Besides Rossi and Bellwether, Dubois mentioned a 'Chef Ramirez' and 'that quiet one from the Scandinavian showcase ... Olsen, I think?' as being part of the game." She quickly cross-referenced their booth locations and contact details. "Ramirez is known for his paella, very gregarious. Olsen ... not so much. Let's try Ramirez first; he seems like more of a talker."

They found Chef Javier Ramirez at his vibrant booth, surrounded by the enticing aroma of saffron and seafood. He was a jovial man with a booming laugh, happy to chat once the lunchtime rush had subsided. When Penny steered the conversation toward the late-night poker game, Ramirez chuckled. "Ah, oui, that game! Dubois, he has the temper of a cornered badger when the cards don't go his way, non?" He confirmed that Dubois, Rossi, Bellwether – briefly – and Chef Astrid Olsen had indeed been playing.

"Was Chef Dubois there the entire time, would you say?" Beth asked, trying to sound casual as she admired a platter of perfectly cooked prawns.

Ramirez paused, his brow furrowing in thought as he sprinkled paprika over a dish. "Now that you mention it ... no. He was losing quite badly to Chef Rossi – she has a surprisingly good poker face, that one. Dubois, he got very ... agitated. Threw his cards down, muttered something about needing 'fresh air' before he said something he'd 'regret,' and stormed off. He was gone for quite a while. An hour, maybe more? Yes, definitely more than an hour. Came back much later, looking even grumpier, just before we all packed it in for the night."

An hour. More than an hour. Right around the estimated time of Nigel Verner's murder. Dubois hadn't just been cooling off; he'd had a significant, unaccounted-for window of time. His poker alibi wasn't just shaky; it had a gaping hole.

The confirmation from Chef Ramirez that Antoine Dubois had been absent from the poker game for over an hour – a crucial window of opportunity on the night of Nigel Verner's murder – sent a fresh jolt of adrenaline through Beth and Penny. Dubois's alibi wasn't just shaky; it was practically nonexistent for the most critical period.

They found Chef Dubois back at his station, barking orders at a flustered-looking assistant who was attempting to polish already gleaming copper pans. The fiery chef was clearly still on edge, his usual theatrical flair tinged with a nervous energy.

"Chef Dubois," Beth began, her voice calm but firm, "we spoke to Chef Ramirez about the poker game."

Dubois spun around, a scowl instantly forming on his face. "So? What of it? I told you, a friendly game. Nothing more."

"Chef Ramirez mentioned you left the game for quite some time," Penny interjected, her gaze steady. "He said you were gone for over an hour. That would have been during the time Mr. Verner was likely killed."

Dubois's face flushed a dangerous shade of crimson, reminiscent of a badly flambéed cherry. He slammed a whisk down on his prep table. "Sacré bleu! Is a man not allowed to take a walk? To clear his head? I was losing! That woman, Rossi, she plays like a sphinx! It was infuriating!" He gesticulated wildly. "So, I went for a walk. Down by the lake, to cool my temper. Is this a crime now? To walk by a lake?"

"A walk that lasted over an hour, Chef?" Beth pressed. "Alone? Did anyone see you?"

"See me? Why would anyone see me? I sought solitude!" he sputtered, though a bead of sweat trickled down his temple. His eyes darted around, avoiding theirs. His claim of a solitary walk felt thin, especially given the location – the very lake where Verner's body was found.

Later, back in the relative sanctuary of the bakery, Penny set COMP-AI to work, digging into any possible connections or recent interactions between Dubois and Verner that might have gone beyond old grudges or bad reviews. "If he was that agitated, it might not just have been about losing at poker," Penny mused. "What if Verner had something on him? Something new?"

It didn't take long for the AI to flag a series of recently deleted emails, retrieved from a backed-up server of a culinary news blog that Verner occasionally freelanced for. The emails, though heavily coded and using pseudonyms, detailed a series of tense negotiations.

"Look at this," Penny breathed, pointing to a decoded message. It was from an account COMP-AI linked to Dubois, desperately trying to arrange a meeting with Verner, referencing a 'mutually beneficial understanding' regarding a 'potentially embarrassing import discrepancy' that Verner had apparently uncovered.

The last email from Dubois, sent just days before the expo, was pleading in tone: "Nigel, we must speak. This could ruin me. There must be a way to resolve this quietly."

Verner hadn't just been a critic; he'd been a threat. And Dubois hadn't just been angry; he'd been desperate to broker a deal to prevent his own ruin.

The revelation that Chef Dubois had been trying to negotiate a secret deal with Nigel Verner over a potentially ruinous "import discrepancy" added a thick layer of motive to his already simmering rage. His hour-long absence from the poker game, his walk by the lake where Verner met his end – it all painted an increasingly damning picture. Beth and Penny shared their findings with Manny, who, despite Galloway's complaints, promised to look into Dubois's import business and any irregularities Verner might have been threatening to expose.

BACK AT SWEETS AND TREATS, the atmosphere was electric. "So, Dubois had a current, pressing reason to silence Verner, not just an old family grudge," Beth summarized, pacing the small back office. "He was desperate."

Sophie, who had been quietly sifting through Dubois's online presence – his restaurant's website, social media, even old culinary school alumni pages – suddenly gasped, her hand flying to her mouth. "Oh my goodness ... look at this." Her voice was barely a whisper, and she looked genuinely shocked.

Beth and Penny rushed to her side, peering at her laptop screen. Sophie had navigated to a cached version of a research database specializing in rare and exotic ingredients, a site often used by avant-garde chefs. Her search history for the site was visible, and one particular query, entered under a username she'd managed to link to Dubois's personal device through a series of digital breadcrumbs COMP-AI had helped uncover, stood out starkly. The search, made just three weeks before the Culinary Expo, was for: "Untraceable organic toxins, rapid incapacitation, culinary applications."

Beneath the search query were links to several obscure botanical articles and ethnobotanical studies, some detailing plants known for their potent, difficult-to- detect neurotoxins.

"Untraceable poisons?" Penny breathed, her eyes wide. "He was researching this weeks ago?"

When confronted by Manny with this new, terrifying piece of evidence later that day – a confrontation Beth and Penny were not privy to but heard about in hushed tones from the officer – Dubois reportedly flew into another apoplectic rage.

He vehemently denied any malicious intent, claiming his research was purely for "gastronomic exploration." He insisted he'd been idly looking into historical uses of rare plants in ancient cuisines, that it was all theoretical, for a new, highly experimental dish he was conceptualizing, something about "challenging the palate with unexpected sensations."

He dismissed the timing as pure coincidence, a chef's

intellectual curiosity. But the explanation, especially in light of everything else, sounded chillingly hollow.

Researching untraceable poisons just before a man he despised, who was threatening to ruin him, ended up murdered?

It was a terrifying thought, Manny shivered as he drove back to town, feeling even more uneasy.

TEN

The air in Chief Galloway's cramped office at the Windy Hollow police station felt thick enough to spread on toast. His face, a mottled shade of plum that Beth privately thought clashed terribly with his uniform, was set in lines of profound irritation. He slammed a sweaty hand down on his already cluttered desk, making a tower of precariously stacked files wobble dangerously.

"Piccott, it's been days!" he boomed, his voice echoing off the peeling paint.

"The Culinary Expo is turning into a three-ring circus, and not the fun kind. We've got national press sniffing around, wondering why we can't solve a simple murder in our own backyard. And what are you bringing me? Theories about flower fibers and burnt notes from a bunch of over-caffeinated chefs!"

Manny stood before the Chief's desk, his expression carefully neutral. Beth and Penny, who been summoned to "share their latest fancies" as Galloway had sarcastically put it, stood slightly behind Manny, feeling the Chief's disdainful gaze settle on them.

"Sir," Manny began, "the evidence we've gathered on Chef Bellwether and Chef Dubois is substantial. Motive, opportunity ..."

"Motive, schmotive!" Galloway interrupted, waving a dismissive hand. "Have you even looked into the obvious? What about Verner's ex-wives? There must be a string of them, right? Critics, like him, they always have angry ex-wives with expensive habits and a grudge. Or a disgruntled former employee he fired dramatically? That's where you find your killer, Piccott, not in a soufflé dish!"

He then turned his attention to Beth and Penny, his expression condescending. "And you two," he said, his voice dripping with sarcasm, "with your ... bakery-based detective work. This isn't one of your cozy little bookstore mysteries, Ms. Whittaker. This is a real murder. Perhaps you should stick to your muffins and tarts, Ms.

Sanders, and leave the actual police work to the professionals."

Beth felt her cheeks flush, but she met his gaze steadily. Penny looked ready to retort, but a subtle shake of Manny's head stopped her.

"Sir," Manny interjected smoothly, drawing Galloway's attention back, "we are pursuing all conventional avenues. However, the victim was here for the expo, surrounded by individuals who had clear, recent conflicts with him. My teams are still conducting thorough searches of the area, including the lakefront. The divers are doing another sweep today. We won't overlook anything."

Galloway grunted, clearly unimpressed with Manny's methodical approach, but not explicitly forbidding the ongoing searches. He just wanted a quick, easy answer, and "angry chefs" or "flower clues" clearly weren't in his book.

Despite Chief Galloway's dismissive attitude toward

their theories and his insistence on pursuing more stereo-
typical, and, in Beth's opinion, far-fetched avenues like
disgruntled ex-wives, Manny Piccott remained steadfast in
his methodical approach.

He knew that thorough police work, not just following
the Chief's whims, was what solved cases. True to his word,
the police divers were once again combing the murky
depths of Cedar Lake, their search grid expanding from the
immediate vicinity of the dock toward the boathouse path
where Nigel Verner's last moments were presumed to have
been.

Beth and Penny had retreated to the bakery, smarting
slightly from Galloway's condescending remarks but more
determined than ever to uncover the truth. Sophie was
expertly handling the afternoon rush, the scent of her
famous chocolate chip cookies a comforting counterpoint to
the grim business at hand. They were discussing the frustrating lack of concrete evidence when Penny's police
scanner app, a somewhat illicit but invaluable tool, crackled
to life.

"Unit 3 to base, we've got something. Repeat, divers
have a find. Sector Gamma, near the old boathouse pilings."
The dispatcher's voice was tinny but clear. Another voice,
likely one of the divers speaking to a shore-based officer,
came through, slightly distorted. "Looks like ... a pen. High
quality, fountain type. Partially buried in the silt. Bringing it
up now."

Beth and Penny exchanged excited, anxious glances. *A
pen?* Galloway would have a field day over this. But the
description "high quality, fountain type" sounded more
promising, more like something a man of Nigel Verner's
stature – or perhaps his killer's – might carry. Minutes later,

which felt like hours, Manny himself called Beth's private line.

"You won't believe this," Manny said, his voice tight with a mixture of frustration and intrigue. "The divers just found a pen in the water near the dock. It's a Montblanc, heavy, expensive. And Beth ... it's got initials. Elegantly calligraphed, right on the silver band. 'J.C.'"

The initials were unmistakable:

J.C.

Julian Croft.

This wasn't just a generic pen; it was a personalized, luxury item, found right where Verner's body had been recovered. Chief Galloway's misguided focus on Croft might have just stumbled into something incredibly significant, albeit for all the wrong reasons. The case against the smooth investor had just taken a very sharp, very incriminating turn.

The discovery of Julian Croft's expensive, initialed Montblanc pen at the murder scene sent a ripple of shock through the makeshift investigation team. While Chief Galloway was undoubtedly already planning his triumphant press conference, Beth and Penny knew that physical evidence, however compelling, was only part of the story.

A motive was still needed, something more concrete than Galloway's vague assertions about "rich men with secrets."

"Okay, so Croft's pen puts him at the scene, or at least his pen was there," Penny said, back in the bakery's back office, the aroma of snickerdoodles doing little to sweeten the grim mood. "But why? What could Verner have had on Croft that would drive a man like him to murder, or to be so careless as to drop his fancy pen during a confrontation?"

Beth recalled Isla Baynard's account of Verner arguing with someone near the boathouse path – the timing and location now aligning ominously with the pen's discovery. "Verner wasn't just a food critic," she mused. "He had a reputation for digging into people's lives, for exposing more than just undercooked fish. What if he stumbled onto something big about Croft's business dealings?"

"Let's find out," Penny declared, her fingers already flying across her COMP-AI keyboard. "COMP-AI, initiate deep background analysis on Julian Croft, focusing on Croft Capital Ventures. Cross-reference with Nigel Verner's known investigative patterns, communication logs from any secondary devices, and any recently accessed or deleted files that might indicate a sensitive investigation on Verner's part."

The AI hummed, its processors whirring through layers of encrypted data, financial reports, and shadowed digital footprints. Minutes ticked by, filled only by the rhythmic click of Penny's keys and Snickers' soft snores from under the table.

Suddenly, a series of sharp beeps broke the silence. "Got something," Penny breathed, her eyes wide as she scanned the screen. "COMP-AI has accessed fragments from a heavily encrypted, secondary cloud storage account Verner used. It looks like Verner wasn't just reviewing Croft's potential restaurant investments ... he was building a full-blown exposé."

She pulled up a series of partially recovered email drafts and notes. "Verner had uncovered evidence suggesting one of Croft's major overseas property developments was mired in serious allegations – bribery, environmental violations, even whispers of forced labor. It was a ticking time bomb, something that could not only destroy

Croft's company but land him in serious legal trouble inter-nationally. Verner's notes indicate he was planning to use it as leverage, or perhaps publish it if Croft didn't comply with some unspoken demand." The motive was no longer speculative; it was stark, dangerous, and potentially explosive.

The recovered notes from Nigel Verner's encrypted cloud storage painted a chilling picture. Julian Croft, the suave and untouchable investor, was facing potential ruin – financial, legal, and reputational – all because of what Verner had unearthed. The air in the bakery's back room crackled with this new, terrifying understanding.

"So, Verner wasn't just an annoying critic to Croft," Beth said, her voice hushed. "He was an existential threat." She looked at Penny and Sophie, their faces reflecting her own shock. "That argument Isla Baynard saw ... by the boathouse path the afternoon before Verner was found. She said Verner was agitated, jabbing his finger, and the other person was mostly obscured. But the timing, the intensity she described ..."

Penny nodded slowly, her eyes fixed on the COMP-AI display showing Verner's damning notes. "It had to be them. Verner confronting Croft, maybe giving him an ultimatum – pay up, pull some strings, or face public annihilation." The pieces were falling into place with horrifying clarity. The secluded boathouse path, the perfect spot for a heated, private confrontation to turn deadly.

Sophie shivered. "And if Croft knew Verner was about to expose him, he'd have every reason to silence him permanently."

The discovery of Croft's initialed Montblanc pen, found precisely in the area where such a fatal struggle might have occurred, now felt less like a convenient piece of evidence for a blustering Chief and more like a cold, hard nail in Julian Croft's coffin.

He had the motive – the most powerful kind – self-preservation.

He had the opportunity, as evidenced by the argument Isla witnessed.

And now, a very personal, very expensive item linked him directly to the place where Nigel Verner had drawn his last breath.

The image of the polished, confident investor suddenly morphed into something far more sinister: a ruthless man cornered, capable of doing anything to protect his empire and his freedom.

The expo, with its glittering displays and gourmet delights, suddenly felt like a gilded cage, and one of its most distinguished guests was now, in their minds, a prime suspect for murder.

ELEVEN

The damning evidence against Julian Croft – the initialed Montblanc pen found at the crime scene coupled with Nigel Verner's notes detailing the explosive exposé he was planning – had shifted the investigation's focus squarely onto the wealthy investor.

Chief Galloway, though initially gleeful at this development, was now feeling the heat. Arresting a man of Croft's stature and influence wasn't like collaring a common criminal; the blowback could be immense if they got it wrong. The Windy Hollow police station, usually a place of sleepy, small-town routine, was buzzing with an unaccustomed tension.

It was into this charged atmosphere that Rick Doyle arrived. He breezed into the station looking like he'd stepped off the cover of a glossy magazine – expensive suit, perfectly coiffed hair, a smile that was all polished confidence and disarming charm.

He introduced himself as a private investigator, retained by Mr. Julian Croft to "assist the authorities in any way possible and ensure a swift resolution to this unfortunate matter, naturally clearing Mr. Croft's good name in the process." His voice was smooth as silk, his handshake firm, and his eyes, Beth noted when she and Penny encountered him leaving Galloway's office, were sharp and missed nothing.

Doyle, it quickly became apparent, was not there to passively observe. He immediately began his own inquiries, his approach a stark contrast to Manny Piccott's quiet diligence. He made a point of seeking out Beth and Penny at Sweets and Treats, ostensibly to gather their impressions as the ones who had discovered Verner's body and who were known to be "community-minded."

"Ladies," he began, accepting a cup of coffee from Beth with a grateful nod, his gaze sweeping appreciatively around the cozy bakery, "Mr. Croft is, of course, devastated by these baseless suspicions. A dropped pen? It's absurd. He's a busy man, easily distracted. Frankly, the man had a confirmed alibi with his valet for the later part of the evening, and this sort of ... passionate crime," he gestured vaguely, referring to the strangulation, "it hardly fits the profile of a calculated businessman like Mr. Croft, does it? It speaks more to a sudden, uncontrolled rage."

He paused, taking a thoughtful sip of coffee. "Let's be candid," he continued, his tone becoming more confidential. "Nigel Verner, while undoubtedly a respected critic whose reviews could make or break careers, was not a popular man. The entire culinary community, it seems, had a complicated relationship with him. Disliked by many, feared by most. It creates a rather wide pool of individuals who might have harbored ... strong feelings."

Doyle then leaned in slightly. "My initial assessment suggests the police might be overlooking more ... volatile individuals, those whose passions run as hot as their stovetops. Individuals with known tempers, perhaps, or those with a history of public animosity toward Mr. Verner. Like that French chef, Dubois? Or even Bellwether, with his rather dramatic past and that interesting botanical history you uncovered."

Doyle's focus was clear: artfully widen the suspect pool to include everyone Verner ever slighted, then subtly narrow it down to anyone but Julian Croft.

Rick Doyle settled into one of the bakery's small, wrought-iron chairs, making it look like a power seat. He leaned forward conspiratorially, lowering his voice, though there was no one else nearby to overhear.

"Between us," he said, his gaze shifting between Beth and Penny, "I've already uncovered a few interesting tidbits that seem to have ... slipped through the cracks of the official investigation."

He took a delicate sip of his coffee, his eyes twinkling as if sharing a delicious secret. "For instance, I've spoken to a rather nervous young catering assistant – poor girl was quite shaken, didn't want to speak to the police initially, but she felt comfortable opening up to me. She was working late near the boathouse path on the night of the murder, clearing some items from a small outdoor reception that had run late. She distinctly remembers seeing a man, rather agitated, pacing near the water's edge around the presumed time of death."

"Did she see his face?" Beth asked, her interest piqued despite her inherent skepticism of Doyle's smooth demeanor. She knew private investigators sometimes embellished, but a new witness was significant.

"Not clearly, no," Doyle admitted with a disarming smile that didn't quite reach his eyes. "It was dark, a bit misty off the lake, and she was, understandably, a bit frightened and trying not to be noticed. But her description ... a man of medium height, dark clothing, rather animated in his gestures, muttering to himself in what she thought might have been French ... She also mentioned he seemed to be wearing a chef's style jacket, though she couldn't be certain of the color in the dim light. It certainly sounds more like our fiery Chef Dubois than a man like Mr. Croft, wouldn't you agree?"

He didn't wait for an answer, smoothly continuing, "And then there's the matter of opportunity. Dubois, as I understand it, had that significant, unaccounted-for gap in his poker alibi that evening. Plenty of time for a ... heated discussion by the lake to turn tragic. A man of his temperament, already furious about losing at cards, perhaps fueled by a little too much wine ..."

Penny, never one to be easily swayed, narrowed her eyes. "That's rather circumstantial, Mr. Doyle. Lots of people were agitated during the expo. And several chefs fit a general description of 'medium height' and 'dark clothing.'"

"Of course, of course," Doyle conceded smoothly, holding up a placating hand. "Just pieces of a larger puzzle. But when you add them to Dubois's known animosity toward Verner, his public outbursts, that rather theatrical note you ladies cleverly uncovered ... a compelling picture begins to emerge, wouldn't you say?"

He then leaned back, steepling his fingers. "Consider also the nature of the attack – strangulation. It's a crime of passion, wouldn't you agree? Up close, personal. Does that sound like a calculated businessman trying to silence a threat? Or more like someone losing control in a fit of rage?" He made it sound as if they were all on the same team, collaboratively solving the crime. Yet, Beth couldn't shake the feeling that he was less interested in finding the truth and more interested in constructing a specific version of it, subtly leading them down a path that conveniently led away from Julian Croft.

LATER, Manny confirmed that Doyle had indeed presented his "findings," including a signed (though somewhat vague) statement from the catering assistant, to Chief Galloway. "The Chief is eating it up with a spoon," Manny said, his voice laced with frustration during a quick call. "Doyle's a smooth talker, and he's feeding Galloway exactly what he wants to hear – a simpler, more emotionally driven suspect than Croft. He even 'hypothesized' how Dubois, in his rage, could have picked up Croft's pen – perhaps Verner had it, or it was dropped earlier – and inadvertently left it at the scene, too consumed by his anger to notice. Galloway's practically ready to redirect the entire investigation toward Dubois. He told me Doyle is a 'real professional who gets results' and that we should all take notes."

The slick PI, it seemed, was already making significant headway in muddying the investigative waters and steering suspicion away from his client.

Rick Doyle, having successfully sown seeds of doubt about Julian Croft and redirected Chief Galloway's attention toward Chef Dubois, didn't let the momentum wane. He made a show of conducting his own meticulous search of the area around the boathouse path, a performance clearly designed for an audience, particularly an audience of one: Chief Galloway. Beth and Penny, observing from a discreet distance near the edge of the police tape (which Doyle had somehow been granted permission to cross), watched with a mixture of suspicion and grudging admiration for his audacity.

Doyle moved with an air of focused intensity, his sharp eyes scanning every inch of the ground, occasionally crouching to examine something innocuous – a fallen leaf, a displaced pebble. Then, with a small, almost theatrical cry of discovery, he stooped near a dense patch of reeds at the water's edge, a spot slightly off the main path that the initial police sweep might have overlooked in the fading light of previous searches.

"Well, now, what have we here?" Doyle called out, loud enough for the nearby officers, and, by extension, Chief Galloway (who was receiving regular updates), to hear. He carefully emerged from the reeds holding a clear evidence bag – one he'd conveniently brought himself – containing a length of what looked like dark, high- strength fishing line. It was thin, almost invisible against the murky green of the reeds, but undeniably strong-looking.

"This was tucked right down at the base of those cattails," Doyle announced to the approaching officer, his voice laced with significance. "Looks like it might have been discarded in a hurry." He held it up for closer inspection. "You know," he mused, as if a sudden thought had struck him, "I recall reading that Chef Dubois is quite the avid angler. Even mentioned in a few culinary magazine profiles that he finds fishing a way to 'de-stress from the pressures of the kitchen.' And this particular type of line ... it's often favored for its strength and low visibility. Ideal for ... well, for many things, I suppose."

The implication was clear and chilling. A strong, nearly invisible line found near the murder scene, potentially linked to a suspect known for fishing and a volatile temper. Chief Galloway, upon hearing of Doyle's "find," was report-

edly ecstatic. This was the kind of tangible, easily understood evidence he craved, far more appealing than complex
botanical fibers or nuanced financial motives.

Rick Doyle hadn't just shifted suspicion; he'd handed
the Chief a new, seemingly perfect thread to pull, one that
led directly to Antoine Dubois.

TWELVE

Rick Doyle's discovery of the high-strength fishing line near the boathouse path had the desired effect on Chief Galloway. The Chief, already swayed by Doyle's smooth presentation and the "eyewitness" account of someone resembling Chef Dubois near the scene, now saw the fishing line as the proverbial smoking gun – or, in this case, the strangling ligature. He immediately ordered Manny Piccott to focus all available resources on Antoine Dubois, practically dismissing Julian Croft despite the damning evidence of the initialed pen and Verner's threatening notes.

Manny, though frustrated by the Chief's abrupt shift and Doyle's manipulative influence, couldn't ignore the fishing line entirely. It was physical evidence, found near the crime scene, and it demanded investigation. He met with Beth and Penny at the bakery, the discarded fishing line carefully bagged and tagged on the small table in the back office, looking incongruous amidst the comforting aroma of cinnamon buns.

"Doyle certainly has a flair for the dramatic, doesn't he?" Penny remarked, nudging the evidence bag with a disdainful finger. "Finds this just when Galloway is losing patience. Convenient."

"Convenient or not, we have to check it out," Manny said, sighing. "Forensics is analyzing it for any trace evidence, but the type of line ... It's a specialized, high-tensile polymer. Very strong, very thin. Could certainly be used as a ligature, and it would be difficult to see, especially at night. Still, I'd expect to see ligature marks on the neck in addition to the fractured hyoid if this was the primary weapon." He looked at Beth. "Regardless, we need to explore all possibilities. Doyle made a point of mentioning Dubois is an avid fisherman. We need to confirm that, and if he uses this specific type of line."

Beth nodded. "Greta Moffat mentioned Dubois often boasts about his fishing prowess at the farmers' market. Says he catches all his own trout for his specials." It was a classic cozy mystery trope – the seemingly innocuous hobby suddenly taking on a sinister light.

The fishing line, on its surface, felt compelling. It offered a tangible weapon, a link to a suspect with a known temper and a fresh motive. Even Penny had to admit, as she examined a close-up photo of the line on her COMP-AI, that it fit the narrative Doyle was weaving a little too neatly.

The question was, was it the truth, or just a well-cast lure?

Armed with the unsettling discovery of the fishing line, Manny, with Beth and Penny providing moral support (and observational skills Manny privately valued more than he let on to the Chief), approached Chef Antoine Dubois. They found him in the midst of a heated phone call in rapid-fire French, gesticulating wildly with a paring knife, his face a mask of indignation. When he finally slammed the phone down, he turned on them, his eyes blazing.

"More questions? Have you not harassed me enough? I am trying to salvage what is left of my reputation after that ... that imbécile Verner tried to destroy it, and now his murder makes us all look like barbarians!"

Manny calmly presented the evidence bag containing the fishing line. "Chef Dubois, this was found near the boathouse path, where Mr. Verner was attacked. It's a specialized, high-strength fishing line. We understand you're a keen fisherman."

Dubois stared at the bag as if it contained a venomous snake. His face, already flushed, deepened to an alarming shade of puce. "Fishing line? And you accuse me? This is an outrage! A fabrication! Yes, I fish! It is a noble pursuit, a way to connect with nature, unlike some who only connect with their own egos!" He spat the last words out, clearly referring to Verner.

"Do you use this type of line, Chef?" Beth asked gently, trying to diffuse his explosive anger.

"How should I know? It is fishing line! There are a million types!" he thundered. "And I was nowhere near that boathouse! I told you, I went for a walk to cool off after that disastrous poker game, but I stayed on the main paths, near the inn gardens! I saw no one, and no one saw me, unfortunately for me now, it seems!" He threw his hands up in exasperation. "Someone is trying to frame me! First the ridiculous burnt note, now this ... this string! It is preposterous! Find the real killer and leave me to my sauces!"

His denial was furious, absolute, and delivered with all the theatrical passion they'd come to expect from him. But beneath the bluster, Beth thought she detected a flicker of genuine fear in his eyes. He was either an incredibly gifted actor or a man unjustly accused, caught in a tightening net.

Chef Dubois's furious denials, while characteristically loud, did little to sway Chief Galloway, especially with Rick Doyle subtly reinforcing the narrative of a temperamental chef pushed too far. Beth and Penny, however, found themselves increasingly uneasy with Doyle's smooth orchestrations. His evidence seemed to appear a little too perfectly, his conclusions a little too neat. They decided to observe the PI more closely.

They found Doyle holding court with a couple of junior officers near the inn's main lobby, pointing toward a detailed floor plan of the Cedar Shore Inn that was framed on the wall, presumably for guest orientation. He was gesturing animatedly, explaining sightlines and potential escape routes from the boathouse area.

Snickers, who had accompanied Beth and Penny, suddenly let out a series of sharp, excited barks, his attention fixed on a half-eaten croissant someone had carelessly dropped near a potted palm. He made a playful lunge for it, his leash momentarily slipping from Beth's grasp.

"Snickers, no!" Beth exclaimed, as the corgi, his leash trailing, made a gleeful dash toward the illicit treat, skidding to a halt near Doyle's expensive shoes and causing a minor commotion. As Doyle and the officers good-naturedly side-stepped the enthusiastic corgi, Penny's keen eyes caught something. Doyle, in redirecting the officers' attention back to the floor plan after the Snickers-induced interruption, didn't just point to the main pathways. He tapped a lesser-known service corridor, then a rarely used staff exit near the kitchens, his finger moving with an assurance that suggested more than a cursory glance at the map.

"If someone wanted to leave the boathouse area

unseen," Doyle was saying smoothly, "this service hallway offers a direct, unmonitored route to the east wing, or even out to the rear parking lot."

Penny's eyes narrowed. For a newcomer to the Cedar Shore Inn, Doyle seemed to possess an almost intimate knowledge of its less obvious nooks and crannies, a familiarity that went beyond what a quick study of a guest map would provide. Beth, watching Doyle's confident, almost stage-managed presentation, felt a growing disquiet. He wasn't just investigating; he was performing, carefully guiding the official police gaze, highlighting certain paths while others remained conveniently in shadow. The feeling that he was expertly manipulating the investigation, rather than simply aiding it, became stronger than ever.

The unease about Rick Doyle's methods and his suspiciously convenient discoveries gnawed at Beth and Penny. While they couldn't pinpoint anything overtly wrong with his finding of the fishing line, his confident navigation of the inn's layout and his subtle steering of the police narrative felt manipulative. Back at Sweets and Treats, as Beth and Penny recounted Doyle's familiarity with the inn, Sophie listened intently, her brow furrowed.

"He just arrived a day ago, right?" Sophie asked. "It's a big inn. Knowing those back corridors and staff exits so well ... it's a bit much for a quick study." While Penny was using COMP-AI to trace the origins and typical retailers of the specific brand of fishing line Doyle had "found," Sophie decided to do her own deep dive, not on the evidence, but on the investigator himself. Her own search engine might not have COMP-AI's raw power, but Sophie had honed her own considerable online research skills during her culinary school days, often needing to find obscure ingredients or techniques.

She started with Rick Doyle's professional website – slick, full of testimonials, but light on concrete details about his past cases. She then moved to news archives, legal databases, and even some of the more shadowy online forums where PIs sometimes discussed (and occasionally disparaged) their colleagues.

For a while, she found nothing but glowing reviews and articles praising his success in high-profile corporate cases. But Sophie was persistent. She started searching for older articles, looking for his name in connection with less savory outcomes or contested investigations.

Suddenly, she let out a small, sharp gasp, her eyes widening as she stared at her screen. "Beth, Penny ... you need to see this." Her voice was hushed, tinged with disbelief. She turned her laptop around. Displayed was an article from a legal journal, dated nearly seven years prior, from a different state. It detailed a high-stakes corporate espionage case where Rick Doyle had been the lead private investigator for the defense. The case had ultimately been dismissed, but not before serious allegations were raised against Doyle himself by the opposing counsel.

The article read: "... questions were raised regarding the provenance of key evidence introduced by Mr. Doyle's team, with opposing counsel formally alleging 'investigative misconduct and potential evidence fabrication'... While no official charges were brought against Doyle due to insufficient proof, the presiding judge noted in his summary a 'disturbing pattern of conveniently discovered materials' that cast a shadow over the proceedings ..."

Beneath that article, Sophie had found links to two other, older cases, both with similar, albeit less formally documented, accusations of Doyle "finding" evidence at just the right moment to exonerate his client or incriminate an opponent.

Rick Doyle, the smooth, professional private investigator, had a history – a pattern of being investigated himself for planting evidence

THIRTEEN

The discovery of Rick Doyle's questionable professional history, with its pattern of conveniently unearthed evidence and accusations of misconduct, sent a shockwave through Beth, Penny, and Sophie. It was one thing to suspect the slick PI of manipulation; it was another entirely to see documented instances of him potentially fabricating evidence. Sophie's findings cast the entire investigation into a new, disturbing light.

The fishing line, so perfectly "found" by Doyle, now seemed less like a clue and more like a carefully planted prop.

Armed with this damning research, Beth and Penny immediately contacted Manny Piccott. The usually unflappable officer was visibly shaken when they laid out Sophie's findings – printouts of the legal journal articles and forum discussions detailing Doyle's past. The "disturbing pattern of conveniently discovered materials" noted by a judge years ago resonated deeply with the current situation in Windy Hollow. For Manny, who prided himself on thorough, ethical police work, the idea that Doyle might be actively corrupting the investigation was a serious blow.

Manny, now backed by Beth and Penny's solid research, confronted Rick Doyle at the Cedar Shore Inn. The PI's usual smooth confidence wavered for the first time when presented with the evidence of his past investigations. His charming smile faltered, replaced by a flicker of something harder, more calculating. Denials were useless in the face of documented history.

"Alright," Doyle finally conceded, his voice losing its silken edge, becoming clipped and professional. "So, my methods have been ... unorthodox in the past. High-stakes cases require creative solutions." He attempted a shrug, but it lacked conviction. "Mr. Croft was understandably concerned about the direction the investigation was taking, with the police focusing on him due to a misplaced pen. He retained me to find the *truth*, to explore other viable suspects the local police might have overlooked."

"And the fishing line, Mr. Doyle?" Manny pressed, his voice cold. "Was that part of your 'creative solution?'"

Doyle sighed, running a hesitant hand through his perfectly coiffed hair, a gesture that seemed almost weary. "Mr. Croft was adamant that Chef Dubois was a likely candidate. The man has a temper, a clear motive. My instructions were to find anything that would solidify that theory, to give the police a ... stronger direction." He paused. "The fishing line, yes. I may have ... enhanced the scene to draw appropriate attention to a plausible theory. My client was desperate, Officer. He wanted results." The admission, though couched in euphemisms, was clear: Rick Doyle had planted the fishing line to frame Antoine Dubois.

Rick Doyle's calm admission of planting the fishing line to incriminate Chef Dubois detonated like a bomb within the Windy Hollow police investigation. When Manny Piccott relayed Doyle's confession to Chief Galloway, the Chief's reaction was volcanic. His face, already prone to a ruddy hue, deepened to an alarming shade of purple usually reserved for his rants about property taxes or the quality of coffee at the station. He paced his small office like a caged bear, his fists clenching and unclenching.

"Planted evidence?!" Galloway roared, his voice bouncing off the thin walls of his office, causing a framed photo of him shaking hands with the mayor to rattle precariously. For once, his anger wasn't directed at Manny. "That ... that charlatan! That slick-haired, city-boy con artist! He waltzes in here, all smiles and expensive shoes, tells me how to do my job, feeds me a line of bull about fishing line and an agitated Frenchman, and I *bought* it!"

The Chief slammed his fist on his desk, scattering pens and paperclips. "He made a fool of me! Of this department!" He was practically vibrating with indignation, not just at Doyle, but at his own gullibility. "And Croft! Hiring a man like that! What in blazes does that say about *him*? Innocent men don't hire snakes to poison the well, Piccott! They cooperate! They trust the process!"

The carefully constructed case against Dubois, built on Doyle's manipulations, crumbled instantly. Galloway, now furious at having been so thoroughly misled, swung his considerable suspicion back toward Julian Croft with the force of a pendulum.

The initialed Montblanc pen, Verner's damning notes about Croft's shady business dealings – all the evidence that Doyle had tried so hard to obscure now blazed with renewed significance in the Chief's eyes.

"Get Croft in here, Piccott!" Galloway bellowed, jabbing a finger toward the door. "Now! If he's hiring people to fabricate evidence, he's desperate. And desperate men do desperate things. I want to know exactly what he paid Doyle to do, and why he felt the need for such ... theatrics!"

Manny found Julian Croft in his luxurious suite at the Cedar Shore Inn, the picture of calm composure as he reviewed documents on a sleek tablet, a half-empty glass of mineral water at his elbow. The late afternoon sun streamed through the window, illuminating dust motes dancing in the air, a stark contrast to the storm brewing within the investigation. When Manny informed him that Rick Doyle had confessed to planting evidence, Croft's carefully maintained facade didn't crack, but a muscle twitched almost imperceptibly in his jaw, and his fingers tightened on the tablet.

"Mr. Croft," Manny began, his voice even, his gaze steady, "Mr. Doyle has admitted to fabricating evidence to implicate Chef Dubois. He stated he was acting on your instructions to find anything that would solidify a case against another suspect."

Croft finally looked up, his eyes cool, assessing. He placed the tablet on the polished mahogany desk with deliberate care. "Officer Piccott," he said, his voice a low, controlled murmur, "let me be unequivocal. I hired Mr. Doyle, a man who came highly recommended, I might add, to find the truth and to protect my interests, which were being unfairly and very publicly targeted. I was desperate, yes. This situation is ... untenable for a man in my position. Reputations are fragile things."

He paused, his gaze unwavering. "But I never *ever* instructed him to manufacture evidence or frame an innocent man. That was Mr. Doyle's own misguided and, frankly, appalling initiative. If he has confessed to such a thing then he acted outside the scope of his engagement and, frankly, has betrayed my trust as well as yours." His denial was smooth, absolute, but the desperation he admitted to, the subtle emphasis on his reputation, hung heavy in the air of the opulent suite.

Julian Croft's denial regarding the planted evidence was delivered with his usual polished conviction, but Manny Piccott wasn't so easily deterred. The investor had admitted to desperation, and Manny sensed a crack in the smooth facade. Chief Galloway, now convinced Croft was a master manipulator, had given Manny carte blanche to press him hard.

"Desperate enough to hire a PI known for ... *creative methods*, Mr. Croft," Manny stated, his voice quiet but insistent. He took a step further into the opulent hotel suite, the scent of expensive cologne and old money faintly discernible. "Desperate enough to want Nigel Verner out of the picture? We know Mr. Verner was investigating your international dealings. We know he had information that could have been catastrophic for you."

Manny laid out the gist of Verner's notes, the threat of exposure, the potential for financial ruin and public disgrace. He watched Croft's face intently, looking for any tell, any flicker of guilt behind the carefully constructed mask of indignation.

Croft listened, his expression unreadable, his hands clasped loosely in his lap. For a long moment, he said nothing, the only sound the distant hum of the hotel's air conditioning and the faint, incongruous chirp of a bird outside the window.

Then, he sighed, a surprisingly weary sound from such a commanding figure, a sound that seemed to carry the weight of years. "Nigel Verner," he began, his voice losing some of its steely edge, becoming softer, almost raw, "had a unique talent for unearthing vulnerabilities, for finding the precise point of leverage. And, yes, he believed he had found one of mine. Not the one you're currently focused on with those ... business speculations, though he certainly would have relished exposing those too, given the chance."

He rose and walked to the window, his silhouette framed against the backdrop of the lake, now tinged with the orange hues of the approaching sunset. "Years ago," Croft continued, his back to Manny, his voice barely above a whisper, "long before Croft Capital Ventures was the entity it is today, I made a smaller, more personal investment. A little bistro, run by a young chef full of promise, a spark of true artistry. Her name was Connie Styles."

The name was new to Manny, but the shift in Croft's demeanor, the sudden weight in his voice, the way he spoke her name with a mixture of reverence and something akin to pain, signaled its profound importance.

"She was brilliant, innovative," Croft said, his voice softer now, almost reflective, a ghost of a smile playing on his lips before vanishing. "Her food ... it was an experience. But then Nigel Verner reviewed her. He didn't just critique her food; he eviscerated her, her spirit. Called her a naive pretender, her creations derivative. The bistro, my investment, it was ruined almost overnight."

He turned back, his face etched with a complex emotion that looked like ... guilt, deep and old. "I cut my losses. Pulled my funding, distanced myself. Advised her to do the same, to disappear, start over if she could. It was a pragmatic business decision at the time; I told myself I couldn't afford to be associated with that kind of spectacular failure, not then, not when I was just starting to build my own name."

He paused, his gaze distant, lost in a past he clearly regretted. "Connie ... she didn't recover. She lost everything. Her passion, her livelihood ... her way. And Verner knew. He knew I'd walked away, knew I'd prioritized my nascent career over her, over basic decency. He'd even hinted recently, with that damnable smirk of his, that such a story of youthful ruthlessness, of a promising talent crushed and abandoned, might make for an interesting sidebar to any other ... difficulties I might be facing. He knew it was a wound I preferred to keep hidden, a ghost I couldn't quite exorcise."

The confession hung in the air, heavy and suffocating. Croft hadn't admitted to murder, but he'd revealed a deep, personal vulnerability, a past act of abandonment driven by financial self-preservation that Nigel Verner could have wielded like a weapon.

It was a powerful motive for wanting the critic silenced, a secret shame that Verner had threatened to drag, kicking and screaming, into the unforgiving light of public scrutiny.

FOURTEEN

Julian Croft's confession about Connie Styles, and the potent blackmail material it represented for Nigel Verner, had once again shifted the sands of the investigation. Rick Doyle's exposure had discredited the case against Chef Dubois, and Chef Bellwether's alibi, while not ironclad, had certainly complicated matters. Now, Croft, with his deeply personal and financially devastating secret, looked like a prime suspect all over again. The whiplash was giving Beth a headache.

"I feel like we're on a merry-go-round of suspects," Beth lamented, back in the familiar comfort of Sweets and Treats. The aroma of baking bread, usually a source of solace, couldn't quite dispel the lingering unease. Snickers, sensing her frustration, nudged her hand with his wet nose. "First Dubois, then Bellwether, now Croft again. Doyle really threw a wrench in everything."

Penny, perched on a stool with a cup of rapidly cooling tea, nodded in agreement. "Doyle definitely muddied the waters, but Croft's story about Connie Styles ... that's a powerful motive. Verner holding that over his head? It's classic blackmail fuel." She sighed. "But, still, strangulation? It felt so personal, so ... hands-on. Does Croft strike you as the type to get his own hands dirty, literally?"

"That's what doesn't quite fit," Beth admitted. "He seems more like the type to hire someone to handle his problems. Like Doyle, but for something more permanent." They needed a fresh perspective, someone who understood the intricate, often brutal, dynamics of the culinary world Nigel Verner had dominated for so long. Their thoughts turned to Chef Elena Rossi. The quiet, dignified Italian chef had been a contemporary of Verner's, had witnessed his rise, and had undoubtedly seen firsthand the wreckage he often left in his wake. She had also, according to Croft, known Connie Styles.

"Let's talk to Chef Rossi," Beth suggested. "She's been through the wringer with Verner herself, but she also seems to have a level head. Maybe she can offer some insight into Verner's other enemies, or even shed more light on this Connie Styles situation from a different angle." Penny agreed. A calm, wise voice was exactly what they needed to cut through the noise of accusations and planted evidence.

They found Chef Elena Rossi at her now quiet booth. The vibrant displays of cannoli and tiramisu from the expo's opening days had been significantly depleted, and she was carefully packing away her remaining pastries and equipment with a gentle, almost reverent touch. Unlike the simmering tension around Chef Dubois or the polished defensiveness of Chef Bellwether, Rossi exuded an air of quiet melancholy, a sadness that seemed to go deeper than just the unfortunate events of the expo.

She offered Beth and Penny a small, weary smile as they approached.

"Signorine Sanders, Whittaker," she greeted them, her

voice soft. "The expo, it has become a very ... somber affair, no?"

"It has, Chef Rossi," Beth agreed. "That's actually why we wanted to talk to you. You knew Nigel Verner for a long time, didn't you? We were hoping you could give us some perspective. He made so many enemies."

Chef Rossi paused in her packing, her gaze distant. She picked up a delicate, unblemished pizzelle, turning it over in her fingers. "Enemies?" she mused. "Nigel did not just make enemies, signorine, he collected them. Like some people collect rare stamps. For him, it was a sport, I think." She sighed, placing the pizzelle carefully into a box. "The culinary world, it looks so glamorous from the outside – the beautiful food, the Michelin stars, the television shows. But beneath the surface, it can be ... a battlefield. Reputations are fragile, built over years of hard work, and can be shattered with a few careless words from a powerful critic."

Penny nodded. "We've certainly seen evidence of that. He seemed to take pleasure in it."

"Pleasure, yes, perhaps," Rossi conceded. "But it was more than that. Nigel understood that true power wasn't just in building someone up, but in the absolute authority to tear them down. He didn't just critique a dish; he critiqued the soul of the chef who made it. He would find a weakness, a vulnerability, and he would press on it until something broke."

She looked at them, her dark eyes filled with a profound understanding. "He destroyed restaurants, yes, but, more than that, he destroyed lives, livelihoods, the very passion that drove people to create. He turned dreams into ash. And, for that, many people would have wished him harm, in their hearts if not with their hands." She spoke of the cutthroat nature of their world not with bitterness, but with a deep, sorrowful wisdom.

Beth felt a chill despite the warm bakery air, Chef Rossi's words painting a stark picture of Nigel Verner's reign. "Julian Croft mentioned someone Verner ... destroyed. A chef named Connie Styles?"

Chef Rossi's expression softened, a flicker of old pain in her eyes. "Ah, Connie," she said, her voice barely a whisper. "Si, I knew her. A long time ago. She was ... a flame. So bright, so talented. She had a little bistro, full of heart. Nigel's review ... it was particularly cruel, even for him. He didn't just criticize her food; he mocked her ambition, her very essence."

Rossi paused, carefully folding a linen napkin. "It broke her, yes, in many ways. Croft, he was her investor then, a young man himself. He pulled out. Many would say it was a sensible business decision. Others ..." She left the sentence unfinished, the implication hanging in the air.

"Croft seemed to feel a great deal of guilt over it," Penny offered.

"Guilt is a heavy ingredient to carry for so many years," Rossi said with a sigh. "Connie ... she never truly recovered from that blow. She tried, for a while, to find her footing again, but something in her had been extinguished. The joy, the spark ... it was gone. She passed away a few years later. Too young." Rossi's eyes misted over for a moment. "The world lost a true artist that day, thanks to Nigel Verner."

Chef Rossi then moved to a small, worn leather satchel she had tucked beside her neatly packed boxes. She rummaged inside for a moment before pulling out an old, slightly creased photograph. "I found this when I was packing for the expo," she said, her voice tinged with nostalgia. "From happier times. Before Nigel." She handed the photo to Beth.

It was a faded color picture of two smiling women in chef's whites, their arms around each other, standing in front of what looked like a charming, rustic restaurant. One was clearly a younger Chef Rossi. The other woman, vibrant and laughing, with kind eyes that held a hint of mischief, must have been Chef Connie Styles. There was a life in her face that made the story of her demise all the more tragic. In the background, slightly out of focus, were the general patrons and ambiance of a bustling little eatery, a snapshot of a dream before it was shattered.

Later that evening, after a long day of emotional revelations and investigative dead ends, Beth and Penny were back at the bakery, tidying up. The old photograph Chef Rossi had given them lay on the counter amidst a scattering of order slips and pastry crumbs. Beth was wiping down the espresso machine, her mind still replaying Julian Croft's confession and Chef Rossi's sorrowful account of Chef Styles.

Penny picked up the photograph again, her brow furrowed in concentration as she studied the faded image of the two smiling chefs and the bustling bistro scene.

Snickers, sensing a lull in the activity, nudged Penny's hand, hoping for a fallen crumb or an ear scratch. Penny absently stroked his head, her gaze still fixed on the photo.

"You know," Penny said slowly, tilting the picture under the warm glow of the bakery lights, "there's something about this photo ... Chef Rossi looks so young, and Chef Styles ... she had such a kind smile. It's heartbreaking what happened to her." She paused, her finger tracing over a slightly blurred figure in the background – a small, dark-haired child who was partially visible near a doorway, a serious little face caught for an instant by the camera. "And this little one here ..." she mused, tapping the image of the child. "Her kid? Looks a bit like Chef Styles."

Beth glanced over, her mind still grappling with Croft's confession and the immediate threats posed by Bellwether or Dubois. "Possibly, Penny," she said, her thoughts elsewhere. "A child caught in all that ... it's heartbreaking to think about. But that was so long ago. We have more pressing leads right now."

She turned back to wiping down the counter. The image of the solemn child in the old photograph was just a single small, sad detail among many.

A tiny, almost invisible thread in a large frustrating carpet that, for now, remained untugged.

FIFTEEN

The unmasking of Rick Doyle as an evidence-planting charlatan had, ironically, done little to simplify the murder investigation of Nigel Verner. If anything, it had made things more complex. Chief Galloway, smarting from being so thoroughly duped, was now laser-focused on Julian Croft, convinced the investor's hiring of Doyle was an admission of guilt by proxy.

Meanwhile, the unsettling questions surrounding Chef Bellwether's botanical past and Chef Dubois's escapades with poison and convenient memory lapses still lingered, casting long, confusing shadows over the entire Culinary Expo. The once- celebratory atmosphere was now thick with suspicion and whispered accusations.

It was amidst this swirling vortex of suspicion that Rick Doyle, remarkably unchastened, reappeared. Beth, Sophie and Penny were in the midst of a mid- morning baking flurry at Sweets and Treats – Beth expertly producing multicolor gum paste sugar flowers for a wedding cake consultation sample with Sophie assisting with delicate painted details, Penny wrestling with a new inventory system on her laptop that seemed determined to categorize book covers as accounting expenses – when the bell over the door chimed, announcing his unwelcome arrival.

He was just as polished as before, his expensive suit immaculate, his tie perfectly knotted, but there was a new tightness around his eyes, a subtle desperation that even his practiced charm couldn't quite conceal.

Snickers, from his usual spot under the counter, let out a low, suspicious growl, a rumbling warning that vibrated through the floorboards. Beth instinctively reached down to rest a calming hand on his head, though her own internal alarm bells were starting to ring. Doyle's presence always seemed to precede a new wave of confusion.

"Ladies, a pleasure, as always," Doyle began, his smile attempting warmth but not quite reaching his eyes. He glanced around the bakery, taking in the trays of cooling pastries and the general hum of activity, perhaps looking for a place to sit, a sign of welcome, but neither Beth, Penny, nor Sophie offered any encouragement. The air, moments before filled with the comforting scent of vanilla and the cheerful clatter of baking tins, grew suddenly cooler, the atmosphere charged.

"I know our last ... interactions ... were less than ideal. A misunderstanding, shall we say, on certain investigative techniques. But I'm still committed to finding the truth in this matter. My professional reputation, after all, is paramount." He sounded almost sincere, if one didn't know his history.

"Is it, Mr. Doyle?" Penny asked, her voice cool as iced tea, not looking up from her screen where she was now pointedly ignoring him and highlighting a particularly egregious error in the inventory software. "Or are you still committed to earning Mr. Croft's rather substantial fee – or what's left of it – regardless of the actual truth?"

Sophie, sensing the tension, quietly moved to stand a little closer to Beth, her usually cheerful expression now wary and observant.

Doyle's smile didn't falter, though a slight flush crept up his neck. "Mr. Croft has, understandably, chosen to ... reevaluate our professional association. However, my own intellectual curiosity regarding this case remains piqued. And I believe I've stumbled upon something that might ... redefine certain aspects of the case. Specifically, regarding Chef Bellwether."

He paused for dramatic effect, his gaze sweeping over them, clearly expecting them to be intrigued, to lean in for his latest revelation. "I've been doing some further, very discreet digging into his financials. It seems his situation is even more precarious than initially thought. I have a source, a very reliable one, who suggests Bellwether was facing imminent foreclosure on his flagship restaurant, something Verner would have undoubtedly delighted in exposing, perhaps even instigated."

He made it sound like a confidential revelation, a crucial piece of the puzzle he was generously sharing, a benevolent act from a dedicated investigator. Beth, however, felt a familiar weariness settle over her; it sounded more like Act Two of Doyle's carefully-crafted misdirection.

Beth stopped her delicate work with the gum paste petals, placing them carefully on a sheet of parchment. She looked at Rick Doyle, her expression unreadable, her patience wearing thin. Penny finally swiveled her chair around, her gaze sharp and direct, her earlier dismissal of him replaced by focused scrutiny.

"Imminent foreclosure, Mr. Doyle? That's quite a

specific and rather dramatic claim. Does this 'reliable source' of yours happen to have any verifiable proof? Or is this another piece of 'creatively enhanced' information, like that conveniently surfaced fishing line you so heroically stumbled upon near the boathouse?" Penny's voice was laced with sarcasm, making no attempt to hide her disbelief.

Doyle's smile flickered, just for an instant, the polished sheen momentarily dulling. "I assure you, ladies, my information is sound. I have in my possession," he tapped his breast pocket significantly, "a copy of a preliminary notice of default that was about to be served to Chef Bellwether. It seems his financial woes run deeper, far deeper, than anyone suspected. Another scathing review from Verner, especially one detailing his impending financial collapse and perhaps hinting at past indiscretions from his 'Bell's Botanicals' days, would have been the final nail in his coffin. Utter ruin."

He exuded confidence, attempting to project an air of unshakable authority, but Beth and Penny, now armed with the knowledge of his past modus operandi, saw through the polished veneer. They recognized the familiar pattern: a new, damning piece of information, conveniently discovered, designed to shift focus squarely onto a chosen target, muddying the waters just enough.

"Mr. Doyle," Beth said, her voice calm but firm, wiping her hands on her apron, her gaze steady. "We know you planted the fishing line near the boathouse to implicate Chef Dubois. Manny Piccott confirmed it. We've also seen the reports from your previous cases, the accusations of investigative misconduct and evidence fabrication. You'll forgive us if we're a little skeptical of any 'new information' you suddenly happen to acquire, especially when it so perfectly fits a narrative you seem determined to push, a narrative that always seems to lead away from your former client."

The PI's carefully-constructed composure began to fray. The charm evaporated, replaced by a cold, appraising stare that held a distinct glint of animosity. "That's a serious accusation, Ms. Sanders. Slanderous, even. I was merely following legitimate leads, trying to assist an incompetent local police force that was clearly out of its depth." His voice was still smooth, but the underlying current was sharp.

"Were you?" Penny challenged, standing up, her hands resting on her hips. "Or were you trying to ensure your client, Mr. Croft, walked away clean, no matter who else took the fall? We won't be your pawns in this, Mr. Doyle. We're not interested in your fabricated documents or your conveniently-coached witnesses. We're interested in the truth, something you seem to have a rather flexible relationship with."

A muscle twitched in Doyle's jaw. His eyes, now devoid of any pretense of friendliness, swept over them, lingering for a moment on Sophie, who stood her ground despite the palpable tension.

"A word of advice, ladies," he said, his voice a low, menacing purr that sent an involuntary shiver down Beth's spine. "Sometimes, it's best to let sleeping dogs lie. People who poke their noses into affairs that don't concern them, who stir up trouble where it's not wanted, often find ... things can get rather unpleasant. Some people, when cornered, especially those with a lot to lose, get what they deserve."

He turned on his heel then, a swift, almost violent motion, and strode out of the bakery, the bell over the door chiming sharply, discordantly, in his wake. He left a chill in the warm, fragrant air, the scent of his expensive cologne suddenly feeling cloying and sinister. His frustration was palpable, and his veiled threat hung between them, ugly and unsettling.

Rick Doyle's abrupt departure left an unnerving silence in the bakery. Beth let out a shaky breath she hadn't realized she'd been holding, her hands slightly trembling as she reached for a discarded piece of gum paste, needing to busy them.

"Well," she said, her voice a little unsteady, trying for a lightness she didn't feel, "that was ... charming. He certainly knows how to make an exit." Snickers, who had been growling softly throughout Doyle's visit, a low thrum of disapproval, finally settled down with a huff, though he kept a wary eye on the door as if expecting the PI to reappear.

Penny, however, looked more energized than intimidated, a familiar glint of determination in her eyes. "He's rattled, Beth. Thoroughly rattled. That threat? That was pure desperation. He knows we're onto him, and he knows we won't just swallow whatever fabricated story he tries to feed us about Bellwether or anyone else."

She began to pace the small space between the counter and the ovens, her bright scarf trailing behind her like a battle standard, her mind clearly working at lightning speed.

"His attempt to point us back toward Bellwether, with that supposed foreclosure notice, was so clumsy, so transparent. It's his signature move, isn't it? Create a new suspect, a new scandal, to draw attention away from the real issue. He's not trying to solve Verner's murder; he's just trying to create enough smoke to cover Croft's tracks, or perhaps, more cynically, to simply earn the rest of his fee by making it look like he's still diligently working the case, even if Croft has officially 'distanced' himself."

She stopped pacing abruptly and looked at Beth, her eyes bright with a dawning realization. "Think about it. Doyle's entire strategy, from the moment he arrived, has been about deflection. First, he plants the fishing line to make Dubois look like the prime suspect. When we, with Manny's help, call him on that, he immediately tries to pivot to Bellwether with some trumped-up financial woes. He's trying too hard to point us away from Croft, or maybe toward the wrong chef entirely."

Penny tapped a thoughtful finger against her lips, her gaze becoming distant. "It makes you wonder, doesn't it? Who benefits most if everyone is looking the wrong way, if the investigation is constantly chasing red herrings, if the truth gets buried under a mountain of fabricated clues and misdirection?"

The question hung in the air, unsettling and profound, suggesting a level of manipulation that went far beyond even Rick Doyle's machinations, hinting at a puppeteer who remained unseen, skillfully pulling strings from the shadows.

SIXTEEN

Rick Doyle's transparent attempt to revictimize Chef Bellwether, coupled with his thinly-veiled threat, had only served to solidify Beth and Penny's conviction that the PI was a desperate man, likely acting on equally desperate instructions. They immediately relayed the encounter to Manny Piccott, their voices tight with indignation over Doyle's audacity.

Manny, already disgusted by Doyle's earlier admission of planting the fishing line, listened grimly, his jaw tightening as they recounted Doyle's words. The PI's continued efforts to muddy the waters, even after being effectively fired by Croft, were deeply troubling. It suggested Doyle was either trying to salvage his exorbitant fee by appearing to still be working the case, or perhaps he was acting on some lingering instruction from Croft to create as much chaos as possible. Or, more chillingly, Doyle might have his own reasons for wanting the investigation to stay away from certain avenues, reasons that had nothing to do with Julian Croft.

"So, Doyle's still trying to earn his paycheck, or maybe

just stir the pot out of spite," Manny said, rubbing his temples wearily. He looked tired, the strain of the high-profile investigation and Chief Galloway's relentless pressure clearly taking its toll. "Galloway wants Croft brought in for another round of questioning. He's convinced Croft is just stonewalling, that the pen is the key. Doyle's latest stunt, trying to pin it back on Bellwether, will only make the Chief dig his heels in harder about Croft's duplicity. He's practically salivating at the thought of a high-profile arrest."

Manny found Julian Croft in the quiet, opulent lounge of the Cedar Shore Inn, nursing a glass of what looked like expensive scotch, the amber liquid catching the late afternoon light. The investor appeared outwardly composed, a financial newspaper resting on the table beside him, but there was a tension in his shoulders, a subtle rigidity in the way he held his glass that hadn't been there before. He looked like a man bracing for an impact.

"Mr. Croft," Manny began, his tone polite but firm, his presence an unwelcome intrusion into the hushed elegance of the lounge. "We need to talk again." He paused, letting the statement settle. "Rick Doyle paid another visit to Ms. Sanders and Ms. Whittaker this morning. He was attempting to feed them information further implicating Chef Bellwether, citing new 'evidence' about his financial situation."

Croft lowered his newspaper slowly, his eyes, usually so quick and assessing, now unreadable, veiled. "Doyle is no longer in my employ, Officer," he stated, his voice a low, carefully modulated baritone. "His methods proved ... incompatible with my standards of discretion and ethics." He took a slow sip of his scotch, his gaze fixed on some distant point beyond Manny.

"Perhaps," Manny conceded, though he doubted

Croft's sudden concern for ethics. "But his persistence is interesting, wouldn't you say? It seems he's still very keen on pointing fingers at anyone but you. One might wonder why he's so determined, even now, to divert attention." Manny let the implication hang in the air, observing Croft for any reaction, any flicker in that polished armor. The investor's mask of cool indifference remained, but Manny thought he saw a flicker of something – weariness? Or was it a deep, unsettling fear? – in the depths of his eyes before it was quickly shuttered away.

Julian Croft set his glass down with a precise, deliberate movement, the ice clinking softly in the sudden silence of the lounge. The sound seemed overloud in the hushed atmosphere. He looked out the large window, his gaze fixed on the tranquil surface of Cedar Lake, a stark contrast to the turmoil brewing within him, and, perhaps, within the investigation itself. When he finally spoke, his voice was low, stripped of its usual confident timbre, revealing a raw vulnerability that surprised Manny, a vulnerability that seemed to cost him a great deal to show.

"Doyle's persistence ..." Croft began, then paused, as if choosing his words with immense care, each one weighed and measured. "It wasn't about Bellwether, Officer. Or Dubois. Not really. Not from my perspective, at least." He turned from the window, his eyes meeting Manny's, and, for the first time, Manny saw not a calculating businessman, but a man genuinely haunted, his composure starting to fray at the edges. "When Nigel Verner was found dead, here, at this expo ... a man I had a very public and very damaging history with regarding another chef ... it stirred up old fears. Fears I've lived with for a very long time, Officer."

He took a deep, unsteady breath. "I hired Rick Doyle, yes. I won't deny that. But my instructions to him were not to frame anyone for Verner's murder, despite what he might have implied to you or anyone else. My primary concern, my *only* concern, was to find out if anyone connected to Connie Styles was here at the expo. If anyone from *her* past, anyone who remembered what Nigel and I did to her, might be seeking some kind of ... retribution."

The admission was startling, a sudden deviation from the expected script of denial and deflection. "Nigel destroyed Connie's career, her life, with my complicity. I stood by and watched it happen. In fact, I facilitated it. I abandoned her when she needed support, when my investment could have saved her bistro, perhaps even her spirit. I chose financial prudence, my own burgeoning career, over loyalty, over common decency." His voice was laced with a profound, self-recriminating guilt that felt utterly genuine.

"I've lived with that decision, with the knowledge of what happened to Connie after I walked away, for years," Croft continued, his gaze dropping to his hands, which were now tightly clasped, his knuckles white. "When Verner died so publicly, so violently, here, in this place teeming with people from our shared world ... I was terrified.

Utterly terrified. Terrified that someone who loved Connie, someone who blamed us both for her suffering and eventual demise, might have finally decided to exact a terrible revenge. First Nigel, then perhaps ... me."

He looked up at Manny, his eyes filled with a genuine, palpable fear that was far more convincing than any of his previous carefully-constructed deflections. "Doyle was supposed to discreetly investigate anyone with ties to Connie, to see if they were present, if they posed a threat to me. His attempts to frame other chefs for Verner's murder were his own misguided and, frankly, reckless interpretations of my desperation. He overstepped, disastrously."

The confession painted Julian Croft in an entirely new light. Not as a cold-blooded killer, but as a man consumed by past guilt and present, paralyzing fear, terrified that the ghosts of his past, and Connie Styles', had finally come to collect their due.

Chief Galloway, when Manny later relayed this new, far more complex confession, was predictably frustrated, his desire for a simple, high-profile arrest thwarted once again. This didn't fit his neat narrative of a ruthless businessman silencing a threat. It was messy, emotional, and pointed away from a straightforward resolution.

Julian Croft's raw confession about Connie Styles, his profound guilt, and his fear of retaliation from someone connected to her past cast a completely different light on his actions. He was no longer the cold, calculating businessman trying to cover up his own crime, but a man haunted by past decisions and terrified of their consequences.

Chief Galloway, predictably, was apoplectic. This new narrative, steeped in old tragedies and personal guilt, was far removed from the straightforward case of a wealthy investor silencing a threat that he had been constructing.

"So now he's a victim of his own conscience?" Galloway had grumbled to Manny, his face a mask of disbelief and irritation. "This whole case is a mess of emotional chefs and terrified millionaires! Get me something solid, Piccott! Something I can take to a judge! I don't care whose ghost is haunting whom!"

BACK AT SWEETS AND TREATS, the mood was somber. Croft's story was tragic, and it resonated with Beth and Penny. The image of Connie Styles, the vibrant chef from Chef Rossi's photograph, destroyed by Verner's cruelty and Croft's abandonment, was heartbreaking. It added another layer of tragedy to Verner's murder, suggesting a cycle of pain and retribution that might have spanned decades.

"So, Croft wasn't worried about Verner exposing his business dealings nearly as much as he was worried about Verner digging into the Connie Styles story or, worse, someone from Connie's past coming after them both," Beth mused, staring out the bakery window at the now-quiet street.

The Culinary Expo was winding down, the brightly colored banners looking a little forlorn in the late afternoon light, their cheerful hues a stark contrast to the dark undercurrents of the investigation.

Penny, who had been uncharacteristically quiet, her brow furrowed in deep thought, suddenly straightened up, a spark igniting in her eyes. She began rummaging through her overstuffed tote bag – a chaotic collection of notebooks, tech gadgets, and emergency snacks – finally pulling out the small, dog-eared notebook she'd used during their earlier interviews. She flipped through the pages, her finger tracing a line of her scribbled notes, her lips moving silently as she reread.

"Wait a minute," she murmured, her finger stopping on a particular entry. "When we spoke to Chef Rossi... she was talking about Connie Styles, about how Verner's review broke her, how she lost everything." Penny's eyes widened, a sudden understanding dawning. "Remember that picture? The kid in the background? The one who looked like Chef Styles?"

She looked up at Beth, the pieces clicking into place

with sudden, startling clarity. "Croft just told Manny he hired Doyle because he was afraid of retaliation from someone connected to *Connie's past*, someone who might blame him and Nigel for her fate." Penny tapped her notebook emphatically, her voice low and urgent. "A mother. A child who would have witnessed their mother's suffering, her destruction, at the hands of Nigel Verner and, by extension, Julian Croft."

The air in the bakery crackled with the unspoken implication, a chilling new possibility taking root. "We've been looking at chefs and investors, at their rivalries and their finances," Penny said, her voice barely above a whisper. "But if Connie had a kid ... who would have just been little when all this happened ... We need to find out what happened to her family. We need to find out what happened to that child."

SEVENTEEN

The previous night's revelation – that Connie Styles had a child who would have witnessed his mother's downfall at the hands of Nigel Verner and Julian Croft – hung heavy in the air of Sweets and Treats. The usual morning bustle of the bakery felt subdued, the clatter of pans and the aroma of baking muffins overlaid with a sense of grim purpose.

Julian Croft's confession had shifted him from a potential killer to a haunted man, but it had also unearthed a new, more poignant motive: a child's grief, potentially festering into an adult's desire for revenge.

"We need to know everything we can about Connie Styles," Beth said, her voice firm as she poured coffee for herself and Penny. Sophie, who had been brought up to speed on Croft's confession, nodded in agreement, her expression somber. "What happened to her after Verner's review, after Croft pulled his investment? And, critically, what became of her child?"

Penny, already at her COMP-AI laptop, grimaced. "That's where it gets tricky. I started digging last night. Professionally, the trail is clear: glowing early reviews for her bistro, The Wandering Vine, then Verner's brutal take-down, followed by financial records showing Croft pulling his investment, and then the bistro's closure. But person-ally? Connie was notoriously private. There are very few interviews, no personal exposés, nothing much beyond her culinary achievements and subsequent professional demise. It's like she vanished from public life after her restaurant failed."

They tried the Windy Hollow Public Library next, hoping Mrs. Abernathy's encyclopedic local knowledge might unearth some forgotten tidbit, perhaps if Connie had relocated nearby. But while Mrs. Abernathy recalled the scandal of Verner's review and the bistro's collapse, she had no information on Connie's personal life or subsequent whereabouts. "A real shame, that was," Mrs. Abernathy had clucked. "Some folks just can't recover from a public shaming like that, especially from a viper like Verner."

Frustrated by the digital and local dead ends regarding Connie's family, Beth sighed. "If anyone would know more about Connie's personal life, especially about her son, it would be Chef Rossi. They were friends. Maybe it's time for another chat with her." It felt like their best, perhaps only, lead to understanding the family Verner had so care-lessly damaged.

Beth and Penny left Sophie looking after the bakery with Snickers *en garde*. They drove the short route to Cedar Shore Inn, where they found Chef Rossi quietly packing the last of her belongings at her now-dismantled expo booth. The vibrant energy of the event had completely faded, leaving behind a sense of melancholy and echoing quiet. Chef Rossi greeted them with a sad smile, her eyes reflecting the weariness they all felt.

"Chef Rossi," Beth began gently, holding out the

creased photograph. "We were looking at this picture you gave us again. You mentioned Connie Styles ... and Julian Croft spoke of her too. He seemed to feel a great deal of guilt."

Rossi nodded slowly, her gaze lingering on the image of her friend. "Connie carried a heavy burden after Nigel's review. And Croft ... well, his actions were those of a young man scared for his own future, perhaps. Understandable, but the consequences for Connie were devastating."

"The little boy in the background of this photo," Penny interjected softly, pointing to the solemn child. "Croft's fear seems to revolve around someone from Connie's past seeking revenge. Was this her child?"

A wistful expression crossed Rossi's face. "Si, that was her boy. Her everything." She sighed. "Connie was a very private woman, especially after ... after everything. She built walls to protect herself, and him. She was a single mother, fiercely devoted. That little one was her reason for getting up in the morning when the world felt too cruel."

"Do you remember his name, Chef?" Sophie asked, her voice full of sympathy.

Chef Rossi shook her head sadly. "It has been so many years, and my friendship with Connie was strongest before ... before the storm. After her bistro closed, she moved away, trying to find peace, to rebuild. We lost touch over time, as people sometimes do. I remember him only as 'Connie's boy,' always serious, always watching. A shadow at her side." She looked at the photo again. "This picture ... it must be from at least twenty-four, maybe twenty-five years ago. He would have been just a little fellow then, perhaps seven or eight."

The information, though not providing a name, was

crucial. A son. A single mother. A timeline. If the photo was roughly twenty-four years old, and Verner's review had come about twelve years after that, Connie's son would have been a young man, acutely aware of his mother's suffering.

With the confirmation from Chef Rossi that Connie Styles was indeed a single mother and that her son would now be a man in his early to mid-thirties, the task ahead became clearer, yet no less daunting. They had a ghost to find, a grown man whose childhood image was their only clue, hidden somewhere within the hundreds, possibly thousands, of faces that had passed through the Culinary Expo.

Back in the bakery, the scent of vanilla and sugar a stark contrast to their grim task, Penny once again fired up her COMP-AI. "Alright," she said, her voice imbued with a fresh sense of purpose. "We're looking for a man, early to mid-thirties. We don't have a name, but we have a child's face to work from, however faded."

She pulled up the image of the boy from Rossi's photo-graph, enlarging the small, serious face as much as possible. "It's a long shot, trying to age-progress this visually and then find a match in a crowd, but COMP-AI has some pretty sophisticated facial recognition and comparison algorithms. We can at least try to narrow down possibilities from the expo attendees."

Beth and Sophie gathered around, peering at the screen. "He had very distinctive, observant eyes, even as a child," Beth noted. "And that serious expression."

The initial trawl through the official expo photo galleries and social media hashtags began. It was an over-whelming flood of images. "The expo was packed even before the murder," Penny sighed, scrolling through endless pictures of guests sampling food, chefs mid-demonstration, and judges looking stern. "After Verner's body was found, the place was crawling with even more people – onlookers, press ... it's like looking for one specific grain of sand on a very crowded beach."

As they meticulously examined photo after photo, a familiar photographer's credit appeared with increasing frequency: "Photo by N. Stern." Sophie was the first to voice what they were all starting to notice. "You know, almost all the really good official shots, the ones with the best clarity and interesting angles, are by Ned Stern. And his Instagram feed, 'N.Stern_Photos,' is full of candids from the expo too."

Penny navigated to Ned's professional Instagram page. It was an impressive collection of artistic shots of food, chefs in action, and atmospheric captures of the event. Amongst them, near the beginning of his expo-related posts, was a selfie. It showed Ned, presumably just after arriving at the Cedar Shore Inn, looking weary but with a hint of an excited smile. His camera bag was slung over one shoulder, and a pile of luggage sat beside him near what looked like the inn's reception desk. The caption was simple: "Finally arrived at Windy Hollow Expo! Can't wait for a shower."

"Okay, so Ned's a prolific and talented photographer," Beth said, pulling Penny's attention back to the task at hand. "But that doesn't help us find a grown-up version of the boy in Rossi's photo."

They spent another frustrating hour scanning faces in the crowd shots, enlarging images, comparing features to the blurry child in the old photograph. COMP-AI, despite its advanced algorithms, struggled to offer any definitive matches based on such limited and aged source material. The sheer number of attendees, the varied lighting, the fleeting expressions – it was an impossible task. Discouragement began to set in.

"This is hopeless," Beth finally said, rubbing her tired eyes. "We're looking for a ghost. Even if he *is* here, picking him out from these crowds based on a twenty-four- year-old blurry photo of a child ..."

Penny, however, wasn't ready to give up. Her fingers tapped restlessly on the keyboard. "Maybe we're going about this the wrong way," she mused. "Instead of trying to find him in the expo photos directly, what if we try to find more information about Connie Styles' death? An obituary might list surviving family members, specifically a son." It was a grim thought, but a logical next step.

The shift in focus from the crowded expo photos to the more targeted search for Connie Styles' final records brought a new, albeit grim, energy to the bakery's back room. "If Connie was as private as Chef Rossi suggested, and if she moved away after the bistro closed, finding an obituary under 'Connie Styles' might be like searching for a specific recipe in a library without a card catalog," Beth commented, watching Penny's fingers fly across the COMP-AI keyboard.

"True," Penny acknowledged, her brow furrowed in concentration. "Professionally, she was 'Connie Styles.' But people often revert to legal names for official records, especially death certificates and obituaries. What if 'Styles' was a professional name, or perhaps her maiden name if she married? COMP-AI, let's broaden the search.

Look for death records for 'Constance S.' or 'Connie S.' with keywords like 'chef,' 'culinary,' 'bistro,' and factor in a likely period of death several years after The Wandering Vine closed. Also, cross-reference with known locations she might have moved to after her restaurant failed."

The AI began its methodical trawl through vast databases. They waited, the silence punctuated by the hum of the laptop and the occasional comforting clink of baking pans from the main bakery where Sophie was holding down the fort. Hours seemed to pass. Several false leads emerged under "Styles," but nothing definitive. The trail for Connie Styles, after her professional life imploded, had gone cold.

"This is tougher than I thought," Penny muttered, frustrated, pushing a stray curl from her eyes. "It's like she completely vanished. What if her legal surname was different altogether? Lots of chefs adopt a catchier name for their career."

She adjusted her search parameters again, instructing COMP-AI to look for any individuals named "Constance" or "Connie" with connections to the culinary world in the estimated timeframe, *regardless* of surname initially, then cross-referencing those hits with details matching what they knew about the closure of The Wandering Vine and her approximate age.

This was a much wider net, requiring more processing power, the digital equivalent of dredging the entire lake. The minutes stretched into an hour, then two, the only sound the whirring of the laptop's fan as COMP-AI sifted through layers of forgotten data.

Sophie had gone home for the night, and Penny was asleep at the counter. Just as Beth was clearing cups, a small, almost apologetic beep sounded from Penny's laptop, a tiny beacon in the digital darkness. Beth's head snapped up. She ran to the laptop, her eyes, tired but suddenly alert, fixed on the screen.

She read the response.

Disappointingly, after all this waiting, the summary stated Connie was survived by "her loving son." No name given.

Another dead end.

EIGHTEEN

Manny left Chief Galloway's office feeling like he'd gone ten rounds with a particularly stubborn mule. The Chief's tunnel vision on Julian Croft was making a thorough investigation nearly impossible. Still, Manny was determined not to let Bellwether or Dubois completely off the hook. He assigned two of his most discreet officers to quietly continue digging into Bellwether's financials and any unusual orders placed by Dubois's restaurant, framing it to Galloway as "tying up loose ends to make the case against Croft airtight." It was a gamble, but one he had to take.

As he was reviewing the preliminary forensics report on Croft's Montblanc pen – which, frustratingly, showed only Croft's own smudged prints and some generic trace elements consistent with being in lake water – his phone buzzed with a text from Beth.

Manny, we haven't gotten much further. We will keep looking, and will let you know if we get anything substantial. Don't want to bother you with wild speculation just yet.

Manny sighed. Beth and Penny's "speculation" had often proven more fruitful than Galloway's pronouncements. He typed a quick reply: *Thanks, Beth. Keep me posted. Any lead is better than the brick walls I'm hitting here.*

He decided to walk over to the Cedar Shore Inn to reinterview some of the staff, hoping for a fresh perspective. As he headed down the main corridor, which was now much quieter as the expo vendors packed up, he nearly collided with Ned Stern. The photographer was laden with camera bags and equipment cases, clearly in the process of departing. Several chefs, also packing, called out goodbyes to him, a testament to the connections he'd made during the event.

"Officer Piccott," Ned said, offering a polite, if slightly weary, nod. He gestured with his chin toward a group of chefs dismantling a particularly elaborate sugar sculpture. "Looks like the circus is finally leaving town. Hopefully, the next culinary event in Windy Hollow will be a little less ... exciting, eh?"

Manny managed a tired smile. "We can all hope for that, Mr. Stern."

Ned adjusted a strap on his shoulder. "Still, quite the send-off for Mr. Verner, wasn't it? Can't say many will miss his particular brand of critique. Guess he finally got a review he couldn't argue with." There was an odd, almost detached amusement in his tone, a slight smirk playing on his lips.

Just as Manny was about to move on, Ned added, a touch self-consciously, "Well, if you'll excuse me, Officer. Duty calls, even at the end. I should probably get one last 'checking out of Windy Hollow' post up for the socials. Keep the followers happy, you know." He gave a slight nod toward his phone.

Manny, attributing Ned's earlier comment about Verner to the dark humor that often surfaces in the wake of a death, merely nodded again. "Safe travels, Mr. Stern." He left the photographer heading toward the reception desk, talking into his phone, taking and posting selfies to his followers.

Manny would never understand people's preoccupation with being in everyone's business all the time.

Meanwhile, he had other priorities to manage. Chief Galloway was increasingly impatient, and, honestly. Manny couldn't blame him. They were no closer to a definitive suspect at this point.

His primary goal was to speak with Isla Baynard again. The innkeeper, with her meticulous attention to detail and her central role in the expo's logistics, might have recalled some small, overlooked detail from the day of the murder or the preceding evening.

He found her in her temporary office, which was now significantly less cluttered as the expo wound down. She looked exhausted but managed a professional smile.

"Officer Piccott," Isla said, gesturing to a chair. "How can I help you today? I trust things are ... progressing?" There was a hopeful lilt in her voice, a clear desire for this whole ordeal to be over.

"We're working on it, Ms. Baynard," Manny replied, trying to sound more confident than he felt. "I just wanted to go over a few things again. Regarding Mr. Croft, specifically. You mentioned seeing him arguing with Mr. Verner near the boathouse path. Could you describe Mr. Croft's demeanor after that argument, if you happened to see him later that day or evening?"

Isla frowned in concentration, tapping a pen against her chin. "Let me think. After that ... unpleasantness by the lake, I believe I saw Mr. Croft in the main lounge much later that evening. He was on his phone, pacing a bit. He seemed ... preoccupied, certainly. Agitated? Perhaps. But then, many people were agitated during this expo, Officer. Nigel Verner had that effect."

She paused. "Actually, there was one small thing. When I saw him in the lounge, he was speaking very brusquely to one of the junior sommeliers who had approached him, something about a wine pairing for a dinner he was apparently hosting in his suite. It was unlike his usual smooth demeanor. He seemed quite sharp with the young man, dismissive. It struck me as odd at the time, given how polished he usually is."

It wasn't much, but it added to the picture of Croft as a man under pressure. Manny thanked Isla for her time. As he walked back toward the station, his phone buzzed again. It was Galloway. "Piccott! Any more on Croft? Have you got him confessing to hiding Verner's toupee yet? I want him sweating! That pen is our golden ticket!"

Manny sighed. Golden tickets and easy answers. That's all the Chief wanted. He thought of Beth's text – "wild speculation." Sometimes, Manny mused, the most important clues weren't golden tickets found under a spotlight, but tiny, overlooked details found far from where everyone else was looking. He just hoped Beth and Penny's intuition would pan out, because he was rapidly running out of official avenues that weren't dead-ending against Galloway's impatience or a suspect's carefully constructed alibi.

AT SWEETS AND TREATS, the lunch rush had subsided, leaving behind the comforting scent of yeast and sugar, and a temporary lull in activity. Sophie, having efficiently cleared the last of the tables, had taken a delighted Snickers out for his afternoon constitutional, leaving Beth and Penny to their increasingly obsessive research.

Last night's research found an obituary for Constance Styles, but frustratingly only read, "...Constance Styles, beloved mother, passed away peacefully after a prolonged illness. She is survived by her loving son."

Beth had scrolled down the digitized page, then back up, her frown deepening. She woke Penny with a curse. "That's it. No first name for the son. Just 'her loving son.'" The information was a breakthrough and a maddening dead end, all at once. They knew Connie had a son. But his identity remained a frustrating, anonymous blank, a ghost they still couldn't name.

Beth was back to looking at expo photos, updated daily by Ned and other participants. The expo was officially over, and there would be no more pictures. In fact, the murderer was likely already gone by now, days after the murder.

Who would stick around after committing murder?

Chefs Rossi, Bellwether and Dubois were all packing their gear, all looking defeated and worse for wear. A few candid shots of Isla definitely did not show her photographic side; Beth wondered how she was doing and if she would ever get over this past week. She reminded herself to bring Isla a Bundt cake the next time she was heading over.

There were excellent shots of the venue itself, the still waters of Cedar Lake, at least pictures that did not include crime scene tape. These at least showed Cedar Shore Inn in a good light, and Windy Hollow as a picturesque small town, ringed with snow dusted mountains. These vistas were part of the reason Beth moved back. The best of North American fresh air and good living.

Except for the victim, of course, Beth thought grimly.

As she scrolled, almost absently at this point, feeling like the answers were just going to slip through their fingers, she noted a picture that made her blink.

What ...?

Beth stopped for a moment, then scrolled back through the expo pictures and the Instagram posts, and reexamined the photos.

She took out her notepad and looked at her notes. Beth's heart started to thud in her chest.

Oh God. We've been wrong this whole time.

She called Manny. Three rings, and it went to voicemail. Hanging up in frustration, she texted:

Manny. Call me immediately. I know who it is. I know who murdered Nigel Verner.

NINETEEN

The text to Manny sent, Beth's hand was still trembling slightly. The pieces had clicked into place with such sudden, shocking clarity that she felt breathless, a cold dread mixing with the adrenaline of discovery.

The bell over the bakery door chimed, a cheerful, incongruous sound, and Beth nearly jumped out of her skin, her tablet clattering onto the counter. Her head snapped up, her heart leaping into her throat, half-expecting Manny to be bursting in, sirens wailing. But it was Penny and Sophie, returning from their walk with Snickers. Penny was mid-laugh, recounting some amusing anecdote to Sophie, her cheeks flushed from the crisp autumn air. Snickers trotted in happily, shaking his ears, his tail wagging a cheerful greeting as he made a beeline for his water bowl.

"Everything alright, Beth?" Penny asked, her laughter dying as she took in Beth's ashen face and wide, haunted eyes. "You look like you've seen a ghost. Or maybe tasted one of Chef Dubois's more experimental concoctions?" she added, attempting a weak joke.

Sophie, too, looked concerned, her bright smile fading.

"Are you okay? Did something happen while we were out? You're white as a sheet."

Beth opened her mouth, ready to pour out her horrifying discovery, the words tumbling over each other in her mind, a chaotic jumble of accusation and dawning certainty. "Penny, Sophie, I ... I think I figured it out. I was looking at the photos again, the expo galleries, and ..."

But before she could explain, before she could share the chilling connection she'd made, the bell over the door chimed again, a sharp, sudden sound that made all three of them start. This time, it wasn't Manny.

Ned Stern stepped into Sweets and Treats, a polite, almost shy smile on his face. He was dressed for travel, in dark, practical clothing, his familiar camera bag slung across his body, a small duffel bag at his feet. The late afternoon sun, slanting through the bakery window, caught his sunglasses perched atop his head, making them gleam for an instant. He seemed to fill the small space, his quiet presence suddenly feeling overwhelmingly large, predatory.

"Hi there," Ned said, his voice soft, unassuming, the same gentle tone he'd used when offering her encouragement about her cake. "Sorry to bother you all, I know you're probably closing up. I was just hoping to pick up a box of those amazing snickerdoodles for the road. Best I've had, seriously. My mother used to make cookies somewhat similar, though not nearly as perfect as yours." He seemed genuinely appreciative, his demeanor entirely at odds with the monstrous image now solidifying in Beth's mind. The casual mention of his mother sent a fresh spear of ice through her.

"Of course, Ned," Beth managed, her voice sounding strained even to her own ears. "Snickerdoodles. How many were you after?"

"Oh, a dozen should do it," he said with a friendly smile. "Enough to get me through the drive."

"Sophie," Beth said, turning to her apprentice. "Could you grab a large bakery box from the back storeroom for Mr. Stern's order? One of the sturdy ones."

Sophie looked puzzled. "But, Beth, we have a whole stack of the usual dozen-count boxes right here under the counter."

"No, no, those won't do," Beth insisted, a little too sharply. Her heart was hammering. She needed Sophie away from the front of the shop. "I want the ones with the reinforced bottoms, the ones we use for heavier orders. They're on the top shelf in the back. And ... and could you take Snickers with you? He looks like he could use a drink of water, and his bowl is back there."

Sophie, though still looking confused by Beth's odd request and sudden, almost panicked, formality, must have sensed the underlying urgency in Beth's tone. She nodded, albeit hesitantly. "Okay, sure." With a soft click of her tongue for Snickers to follow, she headed toward the back room, the corgi trotting happily at her heels, oblivious to the sudden, terrifying tension that had gripped the bakery, leaving an almost unbearable silence in his wake.

With Sophie and Snickers safely out of the immediate vicinity, Beth turned back to Ned, forcing a smile that felt like it might crack her face. Her palms were sweating. Penny watched them, her expression a taut mixture of confusion and dawning apprehension, her gaze flicking between Beth's strained, overly bright face and Ned's oblivious one.

"Your photographs from the expo are really wonderful, Ned," Beth gushed, the words sounding false and overly enthusiastic even to her own ears. She had to keep him talking, keep him disarmed, until Manny arrived. How long would Manny take?

"We were just admiring them online. Penny and I were thinking Sweets and Treats could use a social media boost. Our local tech wizards, Lex and Jay, have helped us out a bit, but we'd love to get some truly professional shots done for our Instagram sometime. What's your process like for food photography? Do you have any special tricks?"

Ned seemed pleased by the compliment, his shoulders relaxing slightly. "Oh, thank you. I mostly do event work, corporate gigs, that sort of thing, but I do enjoy food photography when I get the chance. It's a different kind of challenge." He chuckled softly, a sound that now seemed utterly incongruous with the darkness Beth perceived in him.

"It's all about lighting and composition, really. Finding the right angle to make the food look irresistible, to tell a story with the dish. Sometimes it involves a bit of ... creative staging on my part." He paused, a thoughtful look on his face. "Like with Chef Bellwether's display, for instance. He had those interesting air plants, remember them? Beautiful texture, quite striking, but a bit unruly to photograph effectively. He insisted on having them in almost every shot of his pastries, so I ended up doing a lot of the arranging myself, moving the fronds around to catch the light just so, making sure they complemented the food rather than overwhelming it. He was quite particular about wanting them featured."

Beth's blood ran cold at the casual admission, the innocent-sounding explanation.

He'd handled the Tillandsia. He'd been in direct, prolonged contact with the fibers. The very fibers that had clung to Verner's collar. The fibers that Bellwether himself had cultivated, a signature of his past. Ned had not only been near them; he'd manipulated them, styled them for his shots.

Her phone vibrated quietly in her back pocket. She ignored it, hoping Manny would come find her.

"You certainly have a good eye for detail," she managed, her voice remarkably steady, betraying none of the turmoil inside. "And you seem to have stayed in great shape despite all the tempting food at the expo. Most culinary photographers I know struggle with that aspect of the job." She was fishing, desperately, for any piece of information that would confirm her terrifying theory, anything to keep him talking.

Ned laughed, a natural, easy sound that was terrifyingly normal, chillingly out of place. "Force of habit, I guess. My time in the military drilled a pretty strict diet and exercise regimen into me. Army Rangers, you know," he added, almost as an aside. "Old habits die hard. Thankfully, or I'd probably be as big as a house after a week of sampling all that incredible expo food."

Military. Rangers. The precision. The physical capability. Penny, who had been listening intently, her eyes darting to Ned's easygoing smile, then to Beth's face, suddenly went very still. Her eyes widened almost imperceptibly as the pieces clicked into place for her too – the plant fibers, the expertly choked victim ... The air in the bakery was thick with unspoken terror.

The phone vibrated again, only twice, then stopped.

Manny, take the hint. Where are you?

As if sensing the sudden, almost palpable shift in atmosphere, or perhaps just clumsy from his travels and the weight of his gear, Ned fumbled with the water bottle he'd been holding. It slipped from his grasp, splashing a small puddle onto the worn wooden floor near Penny's feet. "Oh, terribly sorry!" he exclaimed, a flicker of annoyance crossing his face before he smoothed it back into his polite mask. He bent to retrieve the bottle. He straightened up, looking around. "Napkins ...?" he murmured, his gaze sweeping the counter, turning toward where a dispenser sat near the register.

In a movement so swift, so economical, it was almost a blur, he crossed the small space. But instead of reaching for the napkins, his arm shot out, clamping around Penny from behind like a steel band. His other hand came up, pressing something hard – a black knife he pulled out of thin air – against Penny's throat.

Penny gasped, a choked, terrified sound, her eyes wide with shock and fear, her hands flying up to his arm.

"Alright, Beth," Ned Stern said, his voice no longer soft or unassuming, but cold, hard, and chillingly calm. His friendly, boyish demeanor had vanished, stripped away to reveal the focused intensity of a predator.

"The snickerdoodles can wait. How did you find out?"

TWENTY

The air in Sweets and Treats was thick with a terrifying silence, broken only by Penny's ragged breathing and Ned Stern's chillingly calm voice.

Beth's mind raced, her gaze flicking from the hard object pressed against Penny's throat – the base of a wicked knife, she now realized – to Ned's eyes, which were cold and devoid of the gentle warmth they'd held just moments before.

Sophie and Snickers were safe in the back, but Penny was in immediate, mortal danger. Manny was hopefully on his way, but that could be minutes too late. Every second stretched, taut and fragile.

"How did you figure it out?" Ned repeated, his grip tightening slightly on Penny. The pressure made Penny wince, a small, almost inaudible sound.

Beth forced herself to speak, slowly, her voice surprisingly steady despite the tremor in her hands, despite the frantic thumping of her heart. She had to keep him talking, to keep his focus on her, away from Penny.

"The camera strap, Ned." At the use of his given name,

she saw a flicker of surprise, a momentary breach in his icy composure, quickly masked. "When you arrived at the expo, you posted that check-in selfie on Instagram. Your camera bag strap ... it was pristine, new-looking. But in your check-out selfie photo earlier today, I noticed four distinct, parallel scratches across that same strap. Thin, sharp."

She saw his eyes dart instinctively toward his camera bag, still slung over his shoulder, a silent admission.

"Scratches," Beth continued, her voice gaining a fraction more strength, pressing her advantage, trying to keep him engaged, to buy precious seconds. "Like the tines of a fork. Nigel Verner's silver tasting fork, the one Manny found near the dock. He must have raked it across your bag strap when you attacked him. You wanted him to see your face, didn't you? He tried to fight back, but he couldn't hold a candle to a trained Ranger. A desperate, final act. And those coarse, canvas fibers Manny found snagged on the fork? They weren't from Verner's clothes. They were from your camera strap, weren't they? The lab will confirm it."

Ned's expression hardened, a cynical twist to his lips. "Clever. Very observant, Ms. Sanders. Most people just see what's in front of the lens, not the details around it. They see the curated image, not the flawed reality. I lured him out with a promise to take some memorable headshots of him by the lake. The narcissist couldn't resist. When he realized it was the end, he pathetically tried to fight me off with his disgusting tasting fork. He was an easy win."

"And Connie Styles ... or, rather, Connie Stern," Beth pushed on, her gaze unwavering, though inside she was screaming for Manny to arrive. She watched Penny, who was remaining incredibly still, her eyes wide but focused, her breathing shallow. Beth knew Penny was assessing, waiting, just like she was. "The obituary Penny found mentioned she was survived by 'her loving son.' No first name. We thought we hit a dead end. However, we knew she was a single mother. We knew her son would be in his early thirties now. You, Ned, fit the age."

A muscle twitched in Ned's jaw. The mention of his mother, of Connie, seemed to touch a raw nerve. "My mother ... she took the name Styles for her career. Thought it sounded more ... marketable, more chic for a chef on the rise." His voice was laced with a sudden, raw bitterness that was startling. "A lot of good it did her against a monster like Verner, a viper who delighted in crushing talent. She was Constance Stern. A brilliant chef. A kind soul. And he destroyed her. And Croft ... Croft stood by and let him. Watched her light go out and then walked away to count his money."

"You were deployed, weren't you?" Beth guessed softly. "When she was humiliated by Verner's review, when Croft pulled his funding ... and, later, when she died, and broken, before you could get back to help her. You couldn't have known how bad it had gotten."

A deep shadow crossed Ned's face, a profound, soul-deep pain that momentarily eclipsed the coldness. "I was a world away, playing soldier, convinced I was doing something noble, while my mother ... my mother was fighting a battle for her very survival, alone."

His voice cracked, the sound raw and agonizing. "She was too proud, too strong, she wouldn't ask for help, especially from me, not when I was so far away, in danger myself, she'd say. By the time I understood the true depth of her despair, the utter devastation Verner and Croft had wrought ... it was too late. The letters stopped. Then the call came."

He paused, swallowing hard. "The depression. It

consumed me after that. The Army and I, we parted ways. Medically discharged. Photography was the only thing that ... anchored me. A way to observe the world without having to participate in its cruelty."

He shifted his grip on Penny slightly, the knife edge pressed into her throat. Penny made a small, choked sound. Beth's heart leaped. "Don't hurt her, Ned."

"I vowed then," Ned continued, his voice regaining its icy edge, "that Verner and Croft would pay. Not just for her death, but for the slow, agonizing death of her spirit, her passion. I followed Verner to different expos, for years, learning his habits, his routines, his arrogance. I was looking for the perfect way to dismantle him, to expose Croft for the coward he was."

He tightened his grip, causing Penny to wince.

"When Verner insulted your baking, Beth, that day at your booth ... the dish he mocked, your beautiful cake, it was so similar to one of my mother's signature creations, one he'd specifically ridiculed in his review of her bistro. That same sneer, that same casual cruelty ... It just ... snapped something in me. All those years of planning, of waiting for the perfect, cold revenge ... it just boiled over. He had to be silenced. Then. And there."

"And Croft's pen?" Penny managed to rasp out, her voice tight with pain and fear.

"Ah, yes, the pen," Ned said with a mirthless, almost feral smile. "Planting that near Verner's body was almost an afterthought. A little piece of poetic justice. A way to ensure Croft's life became a living hell, to watch him squirm under suspicion, to ruin his reputation just as he'd helped ruin my mother's. I knew there was bad blood between them anyway; it was the perfect misdirection. And that PI he hired, Doyle?"

Ned actually chuckled, a dry, humorless sound.

"What a gift. Doyle was an unexpected but useful tool. Stupid enough to fail so spectacularly in his attempts to frame those other chefs, he only managed to make Croft look even more guilty, more desperate. He did half my work for me when it came to Croft."

Just as Ned finished speaking, the bell over the bakery door chimed loudly, a sudden, sharp intrusion. Manny Piccott stepped inside, his hand instinctively going to his sidearm as he took in the horrifying scene: Ned holding Penny, the knife a vicious weapon against her throat. Manny's eyes widened, his face paling, and he slowly raised his hands in a placating gesture.

"Alright, Ned, let's all stay calm. Let her go. We can talk this through."

The sudden intrusion, the new voice, momentarily broke Ned's intense focus. His head turned slightly toward Manny. In that split second of distraction, a furry brown-and-white missile shot out from the back room, barking furiously, a tiny cannonball of protective rage. Snickers, having heard the commotion or perhaps sensing the acute danger through the closed door, launched himself toward Ned's legs, nipping at his ankles with surprising ferocity for such a small dog, his barks sharp and relentless.

"What the—!" Ned yelped, instinctively flinching and looking down at the unexpected, and surprisingly painful, canine assault. His grip on Penny loosened infinitesimally.

It was the opening Penny had been desperately waiting for. With a sharp exhalation and a sudden, explosive movement that spoke of hours of practice, she twisted her body, driving her weight downward to break his hold. Her elbow connected sharply with his ribs as she spun away, and, with a grunt of pain from Ned, she hooked her leg behind his, using his own momentum against him. Ned stumbled, his eyes wide with surprise and agony, the knife clattering violently to the floor.

Penny looked just as surprised, breathing heavily.

Before he could recover, before he could even process the corgi still attached to his ankle or the woman now free and creating distance, Manny was on him. Years of police training took over, and Manny subdued Ned with swift, practiced efficiency, forcing him to the ground, cuffing his hands securely behind his back.

"Don't hurt him, Manny," Beth said quietly. "He's been hurt enough."

The quiet photographer, Ned Stern, Connie Styles, *née* Stern's, avenging son, was finally apprehended. His carefully constructed facade had shattered, his long- nurtured revenge reaching its bitter, inevitable end.

The reign of Nigel Verner was definitively over, and the ghosts of the past had, in a tragic and violent way, finally found a voice and, perhaps, now, a measure of peace.

TWENTY-ONE

The dramatic capture of Ned Stern in the heart of Sweets and Treats sent ripples of shock, then immense relief, through Windy Hollow. Penny, once the adrenaline subsided, recovered quickly, though not without embellishing her jujitsu takedown with each retelling.

"Honestly, Beth," she'd declared, lounging on a flour sack in the back room the next day, a strategically placed (and entirely unnecessary) bandage on her elbow, "did you see me? It was like a scene from an action movie! The way I used his momentum against him? Pure poetry. Officer Riley naturally wants me to demonstrate at our next class. Snickers was, of course, the true hero, the furry little distraction I needed."

Snickers, basking in the praise, thumped his tail contentedly.

Chief Galloway, predictably, grumbled. Having been so certain about Julian Croft, then briefly about Dubois, the revelation that the quiet, unassuming photographer was the killer, and that a civilian (and her dog) had played a key role in his capture, was a blow to his ego. He mumbled something about "amateur interference" but couldn't deny the outcome.

Manny Piccott, however, was nothing but grateful, shaking Beth and Penny's hands warmly and giving Snickers an official "commendation" in the form of a steak-flavored biscuit.

"We found some pictures of Nigel on Ned's camera taken just after the murder. There is one with Ned posing with Nigel, no doubt satisfied with his long-awaited revenge. It seals the case for us."

"How terrible. Ned was a talented photographer and a veteran - it's a shame he let his sorrow and anger dominate his life," Beth offered.

Julian Croft, cleared of murder but his reputation irrevocably tarnished by his own confession about Connie Styles and his hiring of the disgraced Rick Doyle, quietly left Windy Hollow. The news of his past actions, particularly his abandonment of Connie, spread like wildfire through the tight-knit culinary world, a far more damaging exposé than any Nigel Verner might have penned about his business dealings.

The Culinary Expo, though marred by tragedy, became the talk of the food scene, not just for the murder, but for the complex human drama that had unfolded. Lex and Jay, Penny's tech-savvy contacts, had a field day; their in-depth online coverage of the entire saga, from Verner's critiques to Ned's capture, complete with (tasteful) photos from Ned's own portfolio, went viral, turning Windy Hollow into an unexpected internet sensation.

Amidst the aftermath, Chef Elena Rossi announced she would proceed with a small, private tribute dinner, not for Nigel Verner, but in memory of all chefs whose passion had been unfairly extinguished. She extended a personal invitation to Beth, recognizing a kindred spirit in the young baker who valued craft and heart above all else. It was a quiet acknowledgment – a passing of a torch – that meant more to Beth than any award.

A FEW WEEKS LATER, as the end of summer leaves began to turn vibrant shades of gold and crimson around Windy Hollow, Sweets and Treats was bustling with a different kind of energy. Beth, wanting to give back to the community that had supported her and to create a positive memory after the darkness of the expo, was hosting a "Community Pet Biscuit Baking Workshop."

The idea had been an instant hit. The bakery was filled with cheerful chatter, the scent of peanut butter and oats, and the happy yips of various canine companions, and one very disgruntled-looking cat in a carrier, belonging to Mrs. Higgins.

Hilda Pettigrew and Greta Moffat, self-appointed co-chairs of the "Pumpkin Spice Blend Committee" for the biscuits, were engaged in a spirited, though good-natured, debate over the optimal cinnamon-to-nutmeg ratio. "A pinch more ginger, Hilda, dear!" Greta insisted, waving a measuring spoon. "It needs that *zing* for the discerning canine palate!" Hilda, ever the traditionalist, huffed. "Nonsense, Greta, it'll overpower the subtle notes of the organic oat flour!"

Elliott Yates, the Innkeeper from Windy Hollow Inn, was surprisingly adept at rolling out the dough, his large hands surprisingly delicate. Mayor Augustus Green, having shed his official mayoral demeanor for a flour-dusted apron, was enthusiastically using a bone-shaped cookie cutter, occasionally sneaking a small piece of dough when he thought no one was looking. He even attempted to feed a tiny, unbaked morsel to Snickers, who, after a suspicious sniff, devoured it with gusto, then looked up expectantly for more.

Beth moved through the happy chaos, offering guidance, sharing laughter, her heart feeling lighter than it had in weeks. Sophie was a natural teacher, patiently showing a group of children how to decorate their biscuits with pet-friendly yogurt icing.

Penny was, of course, documenting the entire event for the bakery's now-revitalized Instagram feed, her phone capturing shots of Snickers in a tiny chef's hat she'd fashioned for him.

Later, as the sun began to set, casting a warm glow through the bakery windows, everyone gathered, sipping cider and admiring their trays of freshly baked pet treats. Beth raised her glass.

"To community," she said, her voice full of emotion. "And to good friends, both human and furry." She then added softly, "And to Connie Styles. May her passion for baking, and her love, live on."

There was a quiet murmur of agreement. Chef Rossi, who had made a special trip back for the event, smiled warmly at Beth.

As the last of the workshop attendees departed, laden with bags of biscuits and happy memories, Beth, Penny, and Sophie cleaned up, Snickers happily munching on a slightly misshapen (but perfectly delicious, by his standards) pumpkin biscuit. The bakery, usually a place of focused work, felt imbued with a renewed sense of joy and connection. The murder of Nigel Verner had cast a dark shadow, but it had also, in its own strange way, brought the community closer, highlighting the strength and resilience of Windy Hollow.

Just as Beth was about to lock up, Penny handed her an official-looking envelope that had arrived in the afternoon mail. It was thick, creamy, and bore the embossed insignia of the prestigious National Culinary Guild.

Beth opened it with trembling fingers. Inside, was a beautifully printed invitation. The National Culinary Guild, having heard of her quiet integrity and skill amidst the chaos of the expo (thanks in no small part to Chef Rossi's glowing recommendation and Lex/Jay's viral coverage), was inviting her to be a guest presenter at their upcoming young chefs' symposium, focusing on "The Heart of Artisan Baking."

Tears welled in Beth's eyes. It wasn't just an invitation; it was an acknowledgment, a validation. A new beginning, sweet and full of promise.

Snickers, sensing her emotion, sat squarely at her feet and looked pointedly at the biscuit jar.

Some things, Beth thought with a smile, never changed. And that was perfectly fine with her.

AFTERWORD

A Note from Iris Kingsley

Hello, dear readers!

It warms my heart more than a freshly baked apple pie to know you've spent some time in Windy Hollow with Beth, Penny, and, of course, the ever-charming (and perpetually hungry) Snickers. There's something truly special about small towns, isn't there? That sense of community, where everyone knows your name, your favorite pastry, and perhaps, just perhaps, a secret or two!

For me, writing these stories is like combining all my favorite ingredients: a sprinkle of suspense, a generous cup of friendship, a dash of humor, and always, always, a loyal canine companion by my side (or at my feet, hoping for a dropped crumb). I've always believed that the best mysteries are the ones that feel like coming home, even if home has a few unexpected twists and turns – and maybe a dead body or two!

The world of culinary arts has always fascinated me – the passion, the creativity, the way a simple dish can tell a story or bring people together. And what goes better with a good story than a delicious treat? (You'll find a recipe at the end of the book that I hope brings a little bit of Windy Hollow sweetness into your own kitchen!)

Thank you for joining Beth on her latest adventure. I hope **Murder at the Inn** kept you guessing until the very end and left you with a craving for justice ... and maybe a slice of cake.

Happy reading, and happy baking! Warmly,

Iris Kingsley

(And a happy tail wag from my own furry writing assistant!)

🫐 Summer Berry Shortcake Sheet Cake 🫐

This light, fruity, and picnic-perfect Summer Berry Shortcake Sheet Cake combines the nostalgic charm of strawberry shortcake with the ease and sliceability of a sheet cake.

It features a tender vanilla base, whipped mascarpone cream, and a confetti of fresh berries, this dessert is designed for casual gatherings and sunny celebrations.

It serves 12–16, so it's ideal for family meals with plenty left over for the next day. The townsfolk of Windy Hollow love this snack. So does Snickers!

Ingredients
For the cake:
- 2½ cups all-purpose flour
- 2½ tsp baking powder

- ½ tsp baking soda
- ½ tsp salt
- 1 cup unsalted butter, softened
- 1 ½ cups granulated sugar
- 4 large eggs, room temperature
- 1 Tbsp vanilla extract
- 1 cup buttermilk, room temperature
- Zest of 1 lemon (optional for brightness)

For the whipped mascarpone topping:
- 8 oz mascarpone cheese, cold
- 1 ½ cups heavy whipping cream, cold
- ½ cup powdered sugar
- 1 tsp vanilla extract

For the berry topping:
- 1 ½ cups strawberries hulled and quartered
- 1 cup blueberries
- 1 cup raspberries
- 1 Tbsp lemon juice
- 2 tsp granulated sugar (optional, if berries are tart)

Instructions

1. Prepare the cake:
1 Preheat oven to 350°F. Grease and line a 9x13-inch pan with parchment paper.

2 In a medium bowl, whisk together the flour, baking powder, baking soda, and salt.

3 In a large bowl, cream the butter and sugar until light and fluffy (about 3 minutes). Beat in the eggs one at a time, then add vanilla and lemon zest.

4 Alternate adding the dry ingredients and buttermilk

to the butter mixture, beginning and ending with the dry ingredients. Mix until just combined—do not overmix.

5 Spread the batter evenly in the prepared pan. Bake for 30–35 minutes, or until a toothpick inserted into the center comes out clean.

6 Cool completely in the pan on a wire rack.

2. Make the whipped mascarpone topping:

1 In a chilled bowl, beat mascarpone and heavy cream together until thickened.

2 Add powdered sugar and vanilla; beat to stiff peaks. Keep chilled until ready to use.

3. Macerate the berries:

1 In a medium bowl, toss berries with lemon juice and sugar if needed. Let sit for 10–15 minutes until juicy.

4. Assemble:

1 Spread the whipped mascarpone over the cooled cake.

2 Spoon macerated berries on top just before serving. Drizzle with juices for extra flair.

Optional Tips & Variations:

• Add basil or mint chiffonade over the berries for a sophisticated twist.

• Use a mix of stone fruit (peaches, cherries) alongside berries.

• For portability, top only individual slices with cream and fruit.

I hope you get to enjoy this dessert with your family or loved ones.

Bon appétit!

Love,
    Iris Kingsley

ABOUT THE AUTHOR

About the Author

Iris Kingsley is a firm believer that a good mystery is best paired with a warm cup of tea and a freshly baked treat. She grew up in a close-knit community not unlike Windy Hollow, where the local bakery was the heart of the town and everyone had a story to tell. These early experiences, filled with the comforting aroma of cinnamon and the friendly chatter of neighbors, instilled in her a lifelong love for both storytelling and the culinary arts.

When she's not busy plotting her next cozy mystery or experimenting with new scone recipes, Iris can usually be found exploring local farmers' markets for the freshest ingredients or curled up with a good book, her own loyal (and slightly spoiled) golden retriever, Dexter, snoozing at her feet. Dexter, much like Snickers, serves as her trusted writing companion, chief crumb-taster, and a constant source of inspiration for the furry friends that often find their way into her stories.

Iris loves to hear from her readers and hopes her tales of friendship, community, and, of course, a little bit of murder, bring as much joy to them as they do to her while writing. She currently resides in a charming corner of North America, where the kettle is always on and there's always a new mystery brewing.

ALSO BY IRIS KINGSLEY

Murder in Windy Hollow

Printed in Great Britain
by Amazon